The Book of Wonder

Edward J.
M. D. Plunkett, Lord Dunsany

Contents

THE BOOK OF WONDER
by
Edward J. M. D. Plunkett,
Lord Dunsany

THE BOOK OF WONDER
BY LORD DUNSANY

PREFACE

Come with me, ladies and gentlemen who are in any wise weary of London: come with me: and those that tire at all of the world we know: for we have new worlds here.

THE BRIDE OF THE MAN-HORSE

IN the morning of his two hundred and fiftieth year Shepperalk the centaur went to the golden coffer, wherein the treasure of the centaurs was, and taking from it the hoarded amulet that his father, Jyshak, in the year of his prime, had hammered from mountain gold and set with opals bartered from the gnomes, he put it upon his wrist, and said no word, but walked from his mother's cavern. And he took with him too that clarion of the centaurs, that famous silver horn, that in its time had summoned to surrender seventeen cities of Man, and for twenty years had brayed at star-girt walls in the Siege of Tholdenblarna, the citadel of the gods, what time the centaurs waged their fabulous war and were not broken by any force of arms, but retreated slowly in a cloud of dust before the final miracle of the gods that They brought in Their desperate need from Their ultimate armoury. He took it and strode away, and his mother only sighed and let him go.

She knew that today he would not drink at the stream coming down from the terraces of Varpa Niger, the inner land of the mountains, that today he would not wonder awhile at the sunset and afterwards trot back to the cavern again to sleep on rushes pulled by rivers that know not Man. She knew that it was with him as it had been of old with his father, and with Goom the father of Jyshak, and long ago with the gods. Therefore she only sighed and let him go.

But he, coming out from the cavern that was his home, went for the first time over the little stream, and going round the corner of the crags saw glittering beneath him the mundane plain. And the wind of the autumn that was gilding the world, rushing up the slopes of the mountain, beat cold on his naked flanks. He raised his head and snorted.

"I am a man-horse now!" he shouted aloud; and leaping from crag to crag he galloped by valley and chasm, by torrent-bed and scar of avalanche, until he came to the wandering leagues of the plain, and left behind him for ever the Athraminaurian mountains.

His goal was Zretazoola, the city of Sombelene. What legend of Sombelene's inhuman beauty or of the wonder of her mystery had ever floated over the mundane plain to the fabulous cradle of the centaurs' race, the Athraminaurian mountains, I do not know. Yet in the blood of man there is a tide, an old sea-current, rather, that is somehow akin to the twilight, which brings him rumours of beauty from however far away, as driftwood is found at sea from islands not yet discovered; and this springtide of current that visits the blood of man comes from the fabulous quarter of his lineage, from the legendary, of old; it takes him out to the woodlands, out to the hills; he listens to ancient song. So it may be that Shepperalk's fabulous blood stirred in those lonely mountains away at the edge of the world to rumours that only the airy twilight knew and only confided secretly to the bat, for Shepperalk was more legendary even than man. Certain it was that he headed from the first for the city Zretazoola, where Sombelene in her temple dwelt; though all the mundane plain, its rivers and mountains, lay between Shepperalk's home and the city he sought.

When first the feet of the centaur touched the grass of that soft alluvial earth he blew for joy upon the silver horn, he pranced and caracoled, he gambolled over the leagues; pace came to him like a maiden with a lamp, a new and beautiful wonder; the wind laughed as it passed him. He put his head down low to the scent of the flower, he lifted it up to be nearer the unseen stars, he revelled through kingdoms, took rivers in his stride; how shall I tell you, ye that dwell in cities, how shall I tell you what he felt as he galloped? He felt for strength like the towers of Bel-Narana; for lightness like those gossamer palaces that the fairy-spider builds 'twixt heaven and sea along the coasts of Zith; for swiftness like some bird racing up from the morning to sing in some city's spires before daylight comes. He was the sworn companion of the wind. For joy he was as a song; the lightnings of his legendary sires, the earlier gods, began to mix with his blood; his hooves thundered. He came to the cities of men, and all men trembled, for they remembered the ancient mythical wars, and now they dreaded new battles and feared for the race of man. Not by Clio are these wars recorded; history does not know them, but what of that? Not all of us have sat at historians' feet, but all have learned fable and myth at their mothers' knees. And there were none that did not fear strange wars when they saw Shepperalk swerve and leap along the public ways. So he passed from city to city.

By night he lay down unpanting in the reeds of some marsh or forest; before dawn he rose triumphant, and hugely drank of some river in the dark, and splashing out of it would trot to some high place to find the sunrise, and to send echoing eastwards the exultant greetings of his jubilant horn. And lo! the sunrise coming up from the echoes, and the plains new-lit by the day, and the leagues spinning by like water flung from a top, and that gay companion, the loudly laughing wind, and men and the fears of men and their little cities; and, after that, great rivers and waste spaces and huge new hills, and then new lands beyond them, and more cities of men, and always the old companion, the glorious wind. Kingdom by kingdom slipt by, and still his breath was even. "It is a golden thing to gallop on good turf in one's youth," said the young man-horse, the centaur. "Ha, ha," said the wind of the hills, and the winds of the plain answered.

Bells pealed in frantic towers, wise men consulted parchments, astrologers sought of the portent from the stars, the aged made subtle prophecies. "Is he not swift?" said the young. "How glad he is," said the children.

Night after night brought him sleep, and day after day lit his gallop, till he came to the lands of the Athalonian men who live by the edges of the mundane plain, and from them he came to the lands of legend again such as those in which he was cradled on the other side of the world, and which fringe the marge of the world and mix with the twilight. And there a mighty thought came into his untired heart, for he knew that he neared Zretazoola now, the city of Sombelene.

It was late in the day when he neared it, and clouds coloured with evening rolled low on the plain before him; he galloped on into their golden mist, and when it hid from his eyes the sight of things, the dreams in his heart awoke and romantically he pondered all those rumours that used to come to him from Sombelene, because of the fellowship of fabulous things. She dwelt (said evening secretly to the bat) in a little temple by a lone lakeshore. A grove of cypresses screened her from the city, from Zretazoola of the climbing ways. And opposite her temple stood her tomb, her sad lake-sepulchre with open door, lest her amazing beauty and the centuries of her youth should ever give rise to the heresy among men that lovely Sombelene was immortal: for only her beauty and her lineage were divine.

Her father had been half centaur and half god; her mother was the child of a desert lion and that sphinx that watches the pyramids;--she was more mystical than

Woman.

Her beauty was as a dream, was as a song; the one dream of a lifetime dreamed on enchanted dews, the one song sung to some city by a deathless bird blown far from his native coasts by storm in Paradise. Dawn after dawn on mountains of romance or twilight after twilight could never equal her beauty; all the glow-worms had not the secret among them nor all the stars of night; poets had never sung it nor evening guessed its meaning; the morning envied it, it was hidden from lovers.

She was unwed, unwooed.

The lions came not to woo her because they feared her strength, and the gods dared not love her because they knew she must die.

This was what evening had whispered to the bat, this was the dream in the heart of Shepperalk as he cantered blind through the mist. And suddenly there at his hooves in the dark of the plain appeared the cleft in the legendary lands, and Zretazoola sheltering in the cleft, and sunning herself in the evening.

Swiftly and craftily he bounded down by the upper end of the cleft, and entering Zretazoola by the outer gate which looks out sheer on the stars, he galloped suddenly down the narrow streets. Many that rushed out on to balconies as he went clattering by, many that put their heads from glittering windows, are told of in olden song. Shepperalk did not tarry to give greetings or to answer challenges from martial towers, he was down through the earthward gateway like the thunderbolt of his sires, and, like Leviathan who has leapt at an eagle, he surged into the water between temple and tomb.

He galloped with half-shut eyes up the temple-steps, and, only seeing dimly through his lashes, seized Sombelene by the hair, undazzled as yet by her beauty, and so haled her away; and, leaping with her over the floorless chasm where the waters of the lake fall unremembered away into a hole in the world, took her we know not where, to be her slave for all centuries that are allowed to his race.

Three blasts he gave as he went upon that silver horn that is the world-old treasure of the centaurs. These were his wedding bells.

DISTRESSING TALE OF THANGOBRIND
THE JEWELLER

WHEN Thangobrind the jeweller heard the ominous cough, he turned at once upon that narrow way. A thief was he, of very high repute, being patronized by the lofty and elect, for he stole nothing smaller than the Moomoo's egg, and in all his life stole only four kinds of stone--the ruby, the diamond, the emerald, and the sapphire; and, as jewellers go, his honesty was great. Now there was a Merchant Prince who had come to Thangobrind and had offered his daughter's soul for the diamond that is larger than the human head and was to be found on the lap of the spider-idol, Hlo-hlo, in his temple of Moung-ga-ling; for he had heard that Thangobrind was a thief to be trusted.

Thangobrind oiled his body and slipped out of his shop, and went secretly through byways, and got as far as Snarp, before anybody knew that he was out on business again or missed his sword from its place under the counter. Thence he moved only by night, hiding by day and rubbing the edges of his sword, which he called Mouse because it was swift and nimble. The jeweller had subtle methods of travelling; nobody saw him cross the plains of Zid; nobody saw him come to Mursk or Tlun. O, but he loved shadows! Once the moon peeping out unexpectedly from a tempest had betrayed an ordinary jeweller; not so did it undo Thangobrind; the watchman only saw a crouching shape that snarled and laughed: "'Tis but a hyena," they said. Once in the city of Ag one of the guardians seized him, but Thangobrind was oiled and slipped from his hand; you scarcely heard his bare feet patter away. He knew that the Merchant Prince awaited his return, his little eyes open all night and glittering with greed; he knew how his daughter lay chained up and screaming night and day. Ah, Thangobrind knew. And had he not been out on business he had almost allowed himself one or two little laughs. But business was business, and the diamond that he sought still lay on the lap of Hlo-hlo, where it had been for the last two million years since Hlo-hlo created the world and gave unto it all things except that precious stone called Dead Man's Diamond. The jewel was often stolen, but it had a knack of coming back again to the lap of Hlo-hlo. Thangobrind knew this, but he was no common jeweller and hoped to outwit Hlo-hlo, perceiving not the trend of ambition and lust and that they are vanity.

How nimbly he threaded his way thought he pits of Snood!--now like a botanist, scrutinising the ground; now like a dancer, leaping from crumbling edges. It was quite dark when he went by the towers of Tor, where archers shoot ivory arrows at strangers lest any foreigner should alter their laws, which are bad, but not to be altered by mere aliens. At night they shoot by the sound of the strangers' feet. O, Thangobrind, was ever a jeweller like you! He dragged two stones behind him by long cords, and at these the archers shot. Tempting indeed was the snare that they set in Woth, the emeralds loose-set in the city's gate; but Thangobrind discerned the golden cord that climbed the wall from each and the weights that would topple upon him if he touched one, and so he left them, though he left them weeping, and at last came to Theth. There all men worship Hlo-hlo; though they are willing to believe in other gods, as missionaries attest, but only as creatures of the chase for the hunting of Hlo-hlo, who wears Their halos, so these people say, on golden hooks along his hunting-belt. And from Theth he came to the city of Moung and the temple of Moung-ga-ling, and entered and saw the spider-idol, Hlo-hlo, sitting there with Dead Man's Diamond glittering on his lap, and looking for all the world like a full moon, but a full moon seen by a lunatic who had slept too long in its rays, for there was in Dead Man's Diamond a certain sinister look and a boding of things to happen that are better not mentioned here. The face of the spider-idol was lit by that fatal gem; there was no other light. In spite of his shocking limbs and that demoniac body, his face was serene and apparently unconscious.

A little fear came into the mind of Thangobrind the jeweller, a passing tremor--no more; business was business and he hoped for the best. Thangobrind offered honey to Hlo-hlo and prostrated himself before him. Oh, he was cunning! When the priests stole out of the darkness to lap up the honey they were stretched senseless on the temple floor, for there was a drug in the honey that was offered to Hlo-hlo. And Thangobrind the jeweller picked Dead Man's Diamond up and put it on his shoulder and trudged away from the shrine; and Hlo-hlo the spider-idol said nothing at all, but he laughed softly as the jeweller shut the door. When the priests awoke out of the grip of the drug that was offered with the honey to Hlo-hlo, they rushed to a little secret room with an outlet on the stars and cast a horoscope of the thief. Something that they saw in the horoscope seemed to satisfy the priests.

It was not like Thangobrind to go back by the road by which he had come. No, he went by another road, even though it led to the narrow way, night-house and spider-forest.

The city of Moung went towering by behind him, balcony above balcony, eclipsing half the stars, as he trudged away. Though when a soft pittering as of velvet feet arose behind him he refused to acknowledge that it might be what he feared, yet the instincts of his trade told him that it is not well when any noise whatever follows a diamond by night, and this was one of the largest that had ever come to him in the way of business. When he came to the narrow way that leads to spider-forest, Dead Man's Diamond feeling cold and heavy, and the velvety foot-fall seeming fearfully close, the jeweller stopped and almost hesitated. He looked behind him; there was nothing there. He listened attentively; there was no sound now. Then he thought of the screams of the Merchant Prince's daughter, whose soul was the diamond's price, and smiled and went stoutly on. There watched him, apathetically, over the narrow way, that grim and dubious woman whose house is Night. Thangobrind, hearing no longer the sound of suspicious feet, felt easier now. He was all but come to the end of the narrow way, when the woman listlessly uttered that ominous cough.

The cough was too full of meaning to be disregarded. Thangobrind turned round and saw at once what he feared. The spider-idol had not stayed at home. The jeweller put his diamond gently upon the ground and drew his sword called Mouse. And then began that famous fight upon the narrow way in which the grim old woman whose house was Night seemed to take so little interest. To the spider-idol you saw at once it was all a horrible joke. To the jeweller it was grim earnest. He fought and panted and was pushed back slowly along the narrow way, but he wounded Hlo-hlo all the while with terrible long gashes all over his deep, soft body till Mouse was slimy with blood. But at last the persistent laughter of Hlo-hlo was too much for the jeweller's nerves, and, once more wounding his demoniac foe, he sank aghast and exhausted by the door of the house called Night at the feet of the grim old woman, who having uttered once that ominous cough interfered no further with the course of events. And there carried Thangobrind the jeweller away those whose duty it was, to the house where the two men hang, and taking down from his hook the left-hand of the two, they put that venturous jeweller in his place; so that there fell on him the doom that he feared, as all men know though it is so long since, and there abated somewhat the ire of the envious gods.

And the only daughter of the Merchant Prince felt so little gratitude for this great deliverance that she took to respectability of the militant kind, and became aggressively dull, and called her home the English Riviera, and had platitudes worked in worsted upon her tea-cosy, and in the end never died, but passed away in her residence.

THE HOUSE OF THE SPHINX

WHEN I came to the House of the Sphinx it was already dark. They made me eagerly welcome. And I, in spite of the deed, was glad of any shelter from that ominous wood. I saw at once that there had been a deed, although a cloak did all that a cloak may do to conceal it. The mere uneasiness of the welcome made me suspect that cloak.

The Sphinx was moody and silent. I had not come to pry into the secrets of Eternity nor to investigate the Sphinx's private life, and so had little to say and few questions to ask; but to whatever I did say she remained morosely indifferent. It was clear that either she suspected me of being in search of the secrets of one of her gods, or of being boldly inquisitive about her traffic with Time, or else she was darkly absorbed with brooding upon the deed.

I saw soon enough that there was another than me to welcome; I saw it from the hurried way that they glanced from the door to the deed and back to the door again. And it was clear that the welcome was to be a bolted door. But such bolts, and such a door! Rust and decay and fungus had been there far too long, and it was not a barrier any longer that would keep out even a determined wolf. And it seemed to be something worse than a wolf that they feared.

A little later on I gathered from what they said that some imperious and ghastly thing was looking for the Sphinx, and that something that had happened had made its arrival certain. It appeared that they had slapped the Sphinx to vex her out of her apathy in order that she should pray to one of her gods, whom she had littered in the house of Time; but her moody silence was invincible, and her apathy Oriental, ever since the deed had happened. And when they found that they could not make her pray, there was nothing for them to do but to pay little useless attentions to the rusty lock of the door, and to look at the deed and wonder, and even pretend to hope, and to say that after all it might not bring that destined thing from the forest, which no one named.

It may be said I had chosen a gruesome house, but not if I had described the forest from which I came, and I was in need of any spot wherein I could rest my mind from the thought of it.

I wondered very much what thing would come from the forest on account of the deed; and having seen that forest--as you, gentle reader, have not--I had the advantage of knowing that anything might come. It was useless to ask the Sphinx--she seldom reveals things, like her paramour Time (the gods take after her), and while this mood was on her, rebuff was certain. So I quietly began to oil the lock of the door. And as soon as they saw this simple act I won their confidence. It was not that my work was of any use--it should have been done long before; but they saw that my interest was given for the moment to the thing that they thought vital. They clustered round me then. They asked me what I thought of the door, and whether I had seen better, and whether I had seen worse; and I told them about all the doors I knew, and said that he doors of the baptistry in Florence were better doors, and the doors made by a certain firm of builders in London were worse. And then I asked them what it was that was coming after the Sphinx because of the deed. And at first they would not say, and I stopped oiling the door; and then they said that it was the arch-inquisitor of the forest, who is investigator and avenger of all silverstrian things; and from that they said about him it seemed to me that this person was quite white, and was a kind of madness that would settle down quite blankly upon a place, a kind of mist in which reason could not live; and it was the fear of this that made them fumble nervously at the lock of that rotten door; but with the Sphinx it was not so much fear as sheer prophecy.

The hope that they tried to hope was well enough in its way, but I did not share it; it was clear that the thing that they feared was the corollary of the deed--one saw that more by the resignation upon the face of the Sphinx than by their sorry anxiety for the door.

The wind soughed, and the great tapers flared, and their obvious fear and the silence of the Sphinx grew more than ever a part of the atmosphere, and bats went restlessly through the gloom of the wind that beat the tapers low.

Then a few things screamed far off, then a little nearer, and something was coming towards us, laughing hideously. I hastily gave a prod to the door that they guarded; my finger sank right into the mouldering wood--there was not a chance of holding it. I had not leisure to observe their fright; I thought of the back-door, for the forest was better than this; only the Sphinx was absolutely calm, her prophecy was made and she seemed to have seen her doom, so that no new thing could perturb her.

But by mouldering rungs of ladders as old as Man, by slippery edges of the dreaded abyss, with an ominous dizziness about my heart and a feeling of horror in the soles of my feet, I clambered from tower to tower till I found the door that I sought; and it opened on to one of the upper branches of a huge and sombre pine, down which I climbed on to the floor of the forest. And I was glad to be back again in the forest from which I had fled.

And the Sphinx in her menaced house--I know not how she fared--whether she gazes for ever, disconsolate, at the deed, remembering only in her smitten mind, at which the little boys now leer, that she once knew well those things at which man stands aghast; or whether in the end she crept away, and clambering horribly from abyss to abyss, came at last to higher things, and is wise and eternal still. For who knows of madness whether it is divine or whether it be of the pit?

PROBABLE ADVENTURE OF THE
THREE LITERARY MEN

WHEN the nomads came to El Lola they had no more songs, and the question of stealing the golden box arose in all its magnitude. On the one hand, many had sought the golden box, the receptacle (as the Aethiopians know) of poems of fabulous value; and their doom is still the common talk of Arabia. On the other hand, it was lonely to sit around the camp-fire by night with no new songs.

It was the tribe of Heth that discussed these things one evening upon the plains below the peak of Mluna. Their native land was the track across the world of immemorial wanderers; and there was trouble among the elders of the nomads because there were no new songs; while, untouched by human trouble, untouched as yet by the night that was hiding the plains away, the peak of Mluna, calm in the afterglow, looked on the Dubious Land. And it was there on the plain upon the known side of Mluna, just as the evening star came mouse-like into view and the flames of the camp-fire lifted their lonely plumes uncheered by any song, that that rash scheme was hastily planned by the nomads which the world has named The Quest of the Golden Box.

No measure of wiser precaution could the elders of the nomads have taken than to choose for their thief that very Slith, that identical thief that (even as I write) in how many school-rooms governesses teach stole a march on the King of Westalia. Yet the weight of the box was such that others had to accompany him, and Sippy and Slorg were no more agile thieves than may be found today among vendors of the antique.

So over the shoulder of Mluna these three climbed next day and slept as well as they might among its snows rather than risk a night in the woods of the Dubious

Land. And the morning came up radiant and the birds were full of song, but the forest underneath and the waste beyond it and the bare and ominous crags all wore the appearance of an unuttered threat.

Though Slith had an experience of twenty years of theft, yet he said little; only if one of the others made a stone roll with his foot, or, later on in the forest, if one of them stepped on a twig, he whispered sharply to them always the same words: "That is not business." He knew that he could not make them better thieves during a two-days' journey, and whatever doubts he had he interfered no further.

From the shoulder of Mluna they dropped into the clouds, and from the clouds to the forest, to whose native beasts, as well the three thieves knew, all flesh was meat, whether it were the flesh of fish or man. There the thieves drew idolatrously from their pockets each one a separate god and prayed for protection in the unfortunate wood, and hoped therefrom for a threefold chance of escape, since if anything should eat one of them it were certain to eat them all, and they confided that the corollary might be true and all should escape if one did. Whether one of these gods was propitious and awake, or whether all of the three, or whether it was chance that brought them through the forest unmouthed by detestable beasts, none knoweth; but certainly neither the emissaries of the god that most they feared, nor the wrath of the topical god of that ominous place, brought their doom to the three adventurers there or then. And so it was that they came to Rumbly Heath, in the heart of the Dubious Land, whose stormy hillocks were the ground-swell and the after-wash of the earthquake lulled for a while. Something so huge that it seemed unfair to man that it should move so softly stalked splendidly by them, and only so barely did they escape its notice that one word ran and echoed through their three imaginations--"If--if--if." And when this danger was at last gone by they moved cautiously on again and presently saw the little harmless mipt, half fairy and half gnome, giving shrill, contented squeaks on the edge of the world. And they edged away unseen, for they said that the inquisitiveness of the mipt had become fabulous, and that, harmless as he was, he had a bad way with secrets; yet they probably loathed the way that he nuzzles dead white bones, and would not admit their loathing; for it does not become adventurers to care who eats their bones. Be this as it may, they edged away from the mipt, and came almost at once to the wizened tree, the goal-post of their adventure, and knew that beside them was the crack in the world and the bridge from Bad to Worse, and that underneath them stood the rocky house of the Owner of the Box.

This was their simple plan: to slip into the corridor in the upper cliff; to run softly down it (of course with naked feet) under the warning to travellers that is graven upon stone, which interpreters take to be "It Is Better Not"; not to touch the berries that are there for a purpose, on the right side going down; and so to come to the guardian on his pedestal who had slept for a thousand years and should be sleeping still; and go in through the open window. One man was to wait outside by the crack in the World until the others came out with the golden box, and, should they cry for help, he was to threaten at once to unfasten the iron clamp that kept the crack together. When the box was secured they were to travel all night and all the following day, until the cloud-banks that wrapped the slopes of Mluna were well between them and the Owner of the Box.

The door in the cliff was open. They passed without a murmur down the cold steps, Slith leading them all the way. A glance of longing, no more, each gave to the beautiful berries. The guardian upon his pedestal was still asleep. Slorg climbed by a ladder, that Slith knew where to find, to the iron clamp across the crack in the World, and waited beside it with a chisel in his hand, listening closely for anything untoward, while his friends slipped into the house; and no sound came. And presently Slith and Sippy found the golden box: everything seemed happening as they had planned, it only remained to see if it was the right one and to escape with it from that dreadful place. Under the shelter of the pedestal, so near to the guardian that they could feel his warmth, which paradoxically had the effect of chilling the blood of the boldest of them, they smashed the emerald hasp and opened the golden box; and there they read by the light of ingenious sparks which Slith knew how to contrive, and even this poor light they hid with their bodies. What was their joy, even at that perilous moment, as they lurked between the guardian and the abyss, to find that the box contained fifteen peerless odes in the alcaic form, five sonnets that were by far the most beautiful in the world, nine ballads in the manner of Provence that had no equal in the treasuries of man, a poem addressed to a moth in twenty-eight perfect stanzas, a piece of blank verse of over a hundred lines on a level not yet known to have been attained by man, as well as fifteen lyrics on which no merchant would dare to set a price. They would have read them again, for they gave happy tears to a man and memories of dear things done in infancy, and brought sweet voices from far sepulchres; but Slith pointed imperiously to the way by which they had come, and extinguished the light; and Slorg and Sippy sighed, then took the box.

The guardian still slept the sleep that survived a thousand years.

As they came away they saw that indulgent chair close by the edge of the World in which the Owner of the Box had lately sat reading selfishly and alone the most beautiful songs and verses that poet ever dreamed.

They came in silence to the foot of the stairs; and then it befell that as they drew nearer safely, in the night's most secret hour, some hand in an upper chamber lit a shocking light, lit it and made no sound.

For a moment it might have been an ordinary light, fatal as even that could very well be at such a moment as this; but when it began to follow them like an eye and to grow redder and redder as it watched them, then even optimism despaired.

And Sippy very unwisely attempted flight, and Slorg even as unwisely tried to hide; but Slith, knowing well why that light was lit in that secret chamber and *who* it was that lit it, leaped over the edge of the World and is falling from us still through the unreverberate blackness of the abyss.

THE INJUDICIOUS PRAYERS
OF POMBO THE IDOLATER

POMBO the idolater had prayed to Ammuz a simple prayer, a necessary prayer, such as even an idol of ivory could very easily grant, and Ammuz has not immediately granted it. Pombo had therefore prayed to Tharma for the overthrow of Ammuz, an idol friendly to Tharma, and in doing this offended against the etiquette of the gods. Tharma refused to grant the little prayer. Pombo prayed frantically to all the gods of idolatry, for though it was a simple matter, yet it was very necessary to a man. And gods that were older than Ammuz rejected the prayers of Pombo, and even gods that were younger and therefore of greater repute. He prayed to them one by one, and they all refused to hear him; nor at first did he think at all of the subtle, divine etiquette against which he had offended. It occurred to him all at once as he prayed to his fiftieth idol, a little green-jade god whom the Chinese know, that all the idols were in league against him. When Pombo discovered this he resented his birth bitterly, and made lamentation and alleged that he was lost. He might have been seen then in any part of London haunting curiosity-shops and places where they sold idols of ivory or of stone, for he dwelt in London with others of his race though he was born in Burmah among those who hold Ganges holy. On drizzly evenings of November's worst his haggard face could be seen in the glow of some shop pressed close against the glass, where he would supplicate some calm, cross-legged idol till policemen moved him on. And after closing hours back he would go to his dingy room, in that part of our capital where English is seldom spoken, to supplicate little idols of his own. And when Pombo's simple, necessary prayer was equally refused by the idols of museums, auction-rooms, shops, then he took counsel with himself and purchased incense and burned it in a brazier before his own cheap little idols, and played the while upon an instrument such as that wherewith men charm snakes. And still the idols clung to their etiquette.

Whether Pombo knew about this etiquette and considered it frivolous in the face of his need, or whether his need, now grown desperate, unhinged his mind, I know not, but Pombo the idolater took a stick and suddenly turned iconoclast.

Pombo the iconoclast immediately left his house, leaving his idols to be swept away with the dust and so to mingle with Man, and went to an arch-idolater of repute who carved idols out of rare stones, and put his case before him. The arch-idolater who made idols of his own rebuked Pombo in the name of Man for having broken his idols--"for hath not Man made them?" the arch-idolater said; and concerning the idols themselves he spoke long and learnedly, explaining divine etiquette, and how Pombo had offended, and how no idol in the world would listen to Pombo's prayer. When Pombo heard this he wept and made bitter outcry, and cursed the gods of ivory and the gods of jade, and the hand of Man that made them, but most of all he cursed their etiquette that had undone, as he said, an innocent man; so that at last that arch-idolater, who made idols of his own, stopped in his work upon an idol of jasper for a king that was weary of Wosh, and took compassion on Pombo, and told him that though no idol in the world would listen to his prayer, yet only a little way over the edge of it a certain disreputable idol sat who knew nothing of etiquette, and granted prayers that no respectable god would ever consent to hear. When Pombo heard this he took two handfuls of the arch-idolater's beard and kissed them joyfully, and dried his tears and became his old impertinent self again. And he that carved from jasper the usurper of Wosh explained how in the village of World's End, at the furthest end of Last Street, there is a hole that you take to be a well, close by the garden wall, but that if you lower yourself by your hands over the edge of the hole, and feel about with your feet till they find a ledge, that is the top step of a flight of stairs that takes you down over the edge of the World. "For all that men know, those stairs may have a purpose and even a bottom step," said the arch-idolater, "but discussion about the lower flights is idle." Then the teeth of Pombo chattered, for he feared the darkness, but he that made idols of his own explained that those stairs were always lit by the faint blue gloaming in which the World spins. "Then," he said, "you will go by Lonely House and under the bridge that leads from the House to Nowhere, and whose purpose is not guessed; thence past Maharrion, the god of flowers, and his high-priest, who is neither bird nor cat; and so you will come to the little idol Duth, the disreputable god that will grant your prayer." And he went on carving again at his idol of jasper for the king who was weary of Wosh; and Pombo thanked him and went singing away, for in his vernacular mind he thought that "he *had* the gods."

It is a long journey from London to World's End, and Pombo had no money left, and yet within five weeks he was strolling along Last Street; but how he contrived to get there I will not say, for it was not entirely honest. And Pombo found the well at the end of the garden beyond the end house of Last Street, and many thoughts ran through his mind as he hung by his hands from the edge, but chiefest of all those thoughts was one that said the gods were laughing at him through the mouth of the arch-idolater, their prophet, and the thought beat in his head till it ached like his wrists ... and then he found the step.

And Pombo walked downstairs. There, sure enough, was the gloaming in which the world spins, and the stars shone far off in it faintly; there was nothing before him as he went downstairs but that strange blue waste of gloaming, with its multitude of stars, and comets plunging through it on outward journeys and comets returning home. And then he saw the lights of the bridge to Nowhere, and all of a sudden he was in the glare of the shimmering parlour-window of Lonely House; and he heard voices there pronouncing words, and the voices were nowise human, and but for his bitter need he had screamed and fled. Halfway between the voices and Maharrion, whom he now saw standing out from the world, covered in rainbow halos, he perceived the weird grey beast that is neither cat nor bird. As Pombo hesitated, chilly with fear, he heard those voices grow louder in Lonely House, and at that he stealthily moved a few steps lower, and then rushed past the beast. The beast intently watched Maharrion hurling up bubbles that are every one a season of spring in unknown constellations, calling the swallows home to unimagined fields, watched him without even turning to look at Pombo, and saw him drop into the Linlunlarna, the river that rises at the edge of the World, the golden pollen that sweetens the tide of the river and is carried away from the World to be a joy to the Stars. And there before Pombo was the little disreputable god who cares nothing for etiquette and will answer prayers that are refused by all the respectable idols. And whether the view of him, at last, excited Pombo's eagerness, or whether his need was greater than he could bear that it drove him so swiftly downstairs, or whether as is most likely, he ran too fast past the beast, I do not know, and it does not matter to Pombo; but at any rate he could not stop, as he had designed, in attitude of prayer at the feet of Duth, but ran on past him down the narrowing steps, clutching at smooth, bare rocks till he fell from the World as, when our hearts miss a beat, we fall in dreams and wake up with a dreadful jolt; but there was no waking up for Pombo, who still fell on towards the incurious stars, and his fate is even one with the fate of Slith.

THE LOOT OF BOMBASHARNA

THINGS had grown too hot for Shard, captain of pirates, on all the seas that he knew. The ports of Spain were closed to him; they knew him in San Domingo; men winked in Syracuse when he went by; the two Kings of the Sicilies never smiled within an hour of speaking of him; there were huge rewards for his head in every capital city, with pictures of it for identification--and all the pictures were unflattering. Therefore Captain Shard decided that the time had come to tell his men the secret.

Riding off Teneriffe one night, he called them all together. He generously admitted that there were things in the past that might require explanation: the crowns that the Princes of Aragon had sent to their nephews the Kings of the two Americas had certainly never reached their Most Sacred Majesties. Where, men might ask, were the eyes of Captain Stobbud? Who had been burning towns on the Patagonian seaboard? Why should such a ship as theirs choose pearls for cargo? Why so much blood on the decks and so many guns? And where was the Nancy, the Lark, or the Margaret Belle? Such questions as these, he urged, might be asked by the inquisitive, and if counsel for the defence should happen to be a fool, and unacquainted with the ways of the sea, they might become involved in troublesome legal formulae. And Bloody Bill, as they rudely called Mr. Gagg, a member of the crew, looked up at the sky, and said that it was a windy night and looked like hanging. And some of those present thoughtfully stroked their necks while Captain Shard unfolded to them his plan. He said the time was come to quit the Desperate Lark, for she was too well known to the navies of four kingdoms, and a fifth was getting to know her, and others had suspicions. (More cutters than even Captain Shard suspected were already looking for her jolly black flag with its neat skull-and-crossbones in yellow.) There was a little archipelago that he knew of on the wrong side of the Sargasso Sea; there were but thirty islands there, bare, ordinary islands, but one of them floated. He had noticed it years ago, and had gone ashore and never told a soul, but had quietly anchored it with the anchor of his ship to the bottom of the sea, which just there was profoundly deep, and had made the thing the secret of his life, determining to marry and settle down there if it ever became impossible to earn his livelihood in the usual way at sea. When first he saw it, it was drifting slowly, with the wind in the tops of the trees; but if the cable had not rusted away, it should be still where he left it, and they would make a rudder and hollow out cabins below, and at night they would hoist sails to the trunks of the trees and sail wherever they liked.

And all the pirates cheered, for they wanted to set their feet on land again somewhere where the hangman would not come and jerk them off it at once; and bold men though they were, it was a strain seeing so many lights coming their way at night. Even then...! But it swerved away again and was lost in the mist.

And Captain Shard said that they would need to get provisions first, and he, for one, intended to marry before he settled down; and so they should have one more fight before they left the ship, and sack the sea-coast city of Bombasharna and take from it provisions for several years, while he himself would marry the Queen of the South. And again the pirates cheered, for often they had seen seacoast Bombasharna, and had always envied its opulence from the sea.

So they set all sail, and often altered their course, and dodged and fled from strange lights till dawn appeared, and all day long fled southwards. And by evening they saw the silver spires of slender Bombasharna, a city that was the glory of the coast. And in the midst of it, far away though they were, they saw the palace of the Queen of the South; and it was so full of windows all looking toward the sea, and they were so full of light, both from the sunset that was fading upon the water and from candles that maids were lighting one by one, that it looked far off like a pearl, shimmering still in its haliotis shell, still wet from the sea.

So Captain Shard and his pirates saw it, at evening over the water, and thought of rumours that said that Bombasharna was the loveliest city of the coasts of the world, and that its palace was lovelier even than Bombasharna; but for the Queen of the South rumour had no comparison. Then night came down and hid the silver spires, and Shard slipped on through the gathering darkness until by midnight the piratic ship lay under the seaward battlements.

And at the hour when sick men mostly die, and sentries on lonely ramparts stand to arms, exactly half-an-hour before dawn, Shard, with two rowing boats and half his crew, with craftily muffled oars, landed below the battlements. They were through the gateway of the palace itself before the alarm was sounded, and as soon as they heard the alarm Shard's gunners at sea opened upon the town, and before the sleepy soldiery of Bombasharna knew whether the danger was from the land or the sea, Shard had successfully captured the Queen of the South. They would have looted all day that silver sea-coast city, but there appeared with dawn suspicious topsails just along the horizon. Therefore the captain with his Queen went down to the shore at once and hastily re-embarked and sailed away with what loot they had hurridly got, and with fewer men, for they had to fight a good deal to get back to the boat. They cursed all day the interference of those ominous ships which steadily grew nearer. There were six ships at first, and that night they slipped away from all but two; but all the next day those two were still in sight, and each of them had more guns than the Desperate Lark. All the next night Shard dodged about the sea, but the two ships separated and one kept him in sight, and the next morning it was alone with Shard on the sea, and his archipelago was just in sight, the secret of his life.

And Shard saw he must fight, and a bad fight it was, and yet it suited Shard's purpose, for he had more merry men when the fight began than he needed for his island. And they got it over before any other ship came up; and Shard put all adverse evidence out of the way, and came that night to the islands near the Sargasso Sea.

Long before it was light the survivors of the crew were peering at the sea, and when dawn came there was the island, no bigger than two ships, straining hard at its anchor, with the wind in the tops of the trees.

And then they landed and dug cabins below and raised the anchor out of the deep sea, and soon they made the island what they called shipshape. But the Desperate Lark they sent away empty under full sail to sea, where more nations than Shard suspected were watching for her, and where she was presently captured by an admiral of Spain, who, when he found none of that infamous crew on board to hang by the neck from the yard-arm, grew ill through disappointment.

And Shard on his island offered the Queen of the South the choicest of the old wines of Provence, and for adornment gave her Indian jewels looted from galleons with treasure for Madrid, and spread a table where she dined in the sun, while in some cabin below he bade the least coarse of his mariners sing; yet always she was morose and moody towards him, and often at evening he was heard to say that he wished he knew more about the ways of Queens. So they lived for years, the pirates mostly gambling and drinking below, Captain Shard trying to please the Queen of the South, and she never wholly forgetting Bombasharna. When they needed new provisions they hoisted sails on the trees, and as long as no ship came in sight they scudded before the wind, with the water rippling over the beach of the island; but as soon as they sighted a ship the sails came down, and they became an ordinary uncharted rock.

They mostly moved by night; sometimes they hovered off sea-coast towns as of old, sometimes they boldly entered river-mouths, and even attached themselves for a while to the mainland, whence they would plunder the neighbourhood and escape again to sea. And if a ship was wrecked on their island of a night they said it was all to the good. They grew very crafty in seamanship, and cunning in what they did, for they knew that any news of the *Desperate Lark*'s old crew would bring hangmen from the interior running down to every port.

And no one is known to have found them out or to have annexed their island; but a rumour arose and passed from port to port and every place where sailors meet together, and even survives to this day, of a dangerous uncharted rock anywhere between Plymouth and the Horn, which would suddenly rise in the safest track of ships, and upon which vessels were supposed to have been wrecked, leaving, strangely enough, no evidence of their doom. There was a little speculation about it at first, till it was silenced by the chance remark of a man old with wandering: "It is one of the mysteries that haunt the sea."

And almost Captain Shard and the Queen of the South lived happily ever after, though still at evening those on watch in the trees would see their captain sit with a puzzled air or hear him mutter now and again in a discontented way: "I wish I knew more about the ways of Queens."

MISS CUBBIDGE AND THE DRAGON
OF ROMANCE

THIS tale is told in the balconies of Belgrave Square and among the towers of Pont Street; men sing it at evening in the Brompton Road.

Little upon her eighteenth birthday thought Miss Cubbidge, of Number 12A Prince of Wales' Square, that before another year had gone its way she would lose the sight of that unshapely oblong that was so long her home. And, had you told her further that within that year all trace of that so-called square, and of the day when her father was elected by a thumping majority to share in the guidance of the destinies of the empire, should utterly fade from her memory, she would merely have said in that affected voice of hers, "Go to!"

There was nothing about it in the daily Press, the policy of her father's party had no provision for it, there was no hint of it in conversation at evening parties to which Miss Cubbidge went: there was nothing to warn her at all that a loathsome dragon with golden scales that rattled as he went would have come up clean out of the prime of romance and gone by night (so far as we know) through Hammersmith, and come to Ardle Mansion, and then had turned to his left, which of course brought him to Miss Cubbidge's father's house.

There sat Miss Cubbidge at evening on her balcony quite alone, waiting for her father to be made a baronet. She was wearing walking-boots and a hat and a lownecked evening dress; for a painter was but just now painting her portrait and neither she nor the painter saw anything odd in the strange combination. She did not notice the roar of the dragon's golden scales, nor distinguish above the manifold lights of London the small, red glare of his eyes. He suddenly lifted his head, a blaze of gold, over the balcony; he did not appear a yellow dragon then, for his glistening scales reflected the beauty that London puts upon her only at evening and night. She screamed, but to no knight, nor knew what knight to call on, nor guessed where were the dragons' overthrowers of far, romantic days, nor what mightier game they chased, or what wars they waged; perchance they were busy even then arming for Armageddon.

* * * * *

Out of the balcony of her father's house in Prince of Wales' Square, the painted dark-green balcony that grew blacker every year, the dragon lifted Miss Cubbidge and spread his rattling wings, and London fell away like an old fashion. And England fell away, and the smoke of its factories, and the round material world that goes humming round the sun vexed and pursued by time, until there appeared the eternal and ancient lands of Romance lying low by mystical seas.

You had not pictured Miss Cubbidge stroking the golden head of one of the dragons of song with one hand idly, while with the other she sometime played with pearls brought up from lonely places of the sea. They filled huge haliotis shells with pearls and laid them there beside her, they brought her emeralds which she set to flash among the tresses of her long black hair, they brought her threaded sapphires for her cloak: all this the princes of fable did and the elves and the gnomes of myth. And partly she still lived, and partly she was one with long-ago and with those sacred tales that nurses tell, when all their children are good, and evening has come, and the fire is burning well, and the soft pat-pat of the snowflakes on the pane is like the furtive tread of fearful things in old, enchanted woods. If at first she missed those dainty novelties among which she was reared, the old, sufficient song of the mystical sea singing of faery lore at first soothed and at last consoled her. Even, she forgot those advertisements of pills that are so dear to England; even, she forgot political cant and the things that one discusses and the things that one does not, and had perforce to contend herself with seeing sailing by huge golden-laden galleons with treasure for Madrid, and the merry skull-and-cross-bones of the pirateers, and the tiny nautilus setting out to sea, and ships of heroes trafficking in romance or of princes seeking for enchanted isles.

It was not by chains that the dragon kept her there, but by one of the spells of old. To one to whom the facilities of the daily Press had for so long been accorded spells would have palled--you would have said--and galleons after a time and all things out-of-date. After a time. But whether the centuries passed her or whether the years or whether no time at all, she did not know. If any thing indicated the passing of time it was the rhythm of elfin horns blowing upon the heights. If the centuries went by her the spell that bound her gave her also perennial youth, and kept alight for ever the lantern by her side, and saved from decay the marble palace facing the mystical sea. And if no time went by her there at all, her single moment on those marvellous coasts was turned as it were to a crystal reflecting a thousand scenes. If it was all a dream, it was a dream that knew no morning and no fading away. The tide roamed on and whispered of master and of myth, while near that captive lady, asleep in his marble tank the golden dragon dreamed: and a little way out from the coast all that the dragon dreamed showed faintly in the mist that lay over the sea. He never dreamed of any rescuing knight. So long as he dreamed, it was twilight; but when he came up nimbly out of his tank night fell and starlight glistened on the dripping, golden scales.

There he and his captive either defeated Time or never encountered him at all; while, in the world we know, raged Roncesvalles or battles yet to be--I know not to what part of the shore of Romance he bore her. Perhaps she became one of those princesses of whom fable loves to tell, but let it suffice that there she lived by the sea: and kings ruled, and Demons ruled, and kings came again, and many cities returned to their native dust, and still she abided there, and still her marble palace passed not away nor the power that there was in the dragon's spell.

And only once did there ever come to her a message from the world that of old she knew. It came in a pearly ship across the mystical sea; it was from an old school-friend that she had had in Putney, merely a note, no more, in a little, neat, round hand: it said, "It is not Proper for you to be there alone."

THE QUEST OF THE QUEEN'S TEARS

SYLVIA, Queen of the Woods, in her woodland palace, held court, and made a mockery of her suitors. She would sing to them, she said, she would give them banquets, she would tell them tales of legendary days, her jugglers should caper before them, her armies salute them, her fools crack jests with them and make whimsical quips, only she could not love them.

This was not the way, they said, to treat princes in their splendor and mysterious troubadours concealing kingly names; it was not in accordance with fable; myth had no precedent for it. She should have thrown her glove, they said, into some lion's den, she should have asked for a score of venomous heads of the serpents of Licantara, or demanded the death of any notable dragon, or sent them all upon some deadly quest, but that she could not love them--! It was unheard of--it had no parallel in the annals of romance.

And then she said that if they must needs have a quest she would offer her hand to him who first should move her to tears: and the quest should be called, for reference in histories or song, the Quest of the Queen's Tears, and he that achieved them she would wed, be he only a petty duke of lands unknown to romance.

And many were moved to anger, for they hoped for some bloody quest; but the old lords chamberlain said, as they muttered among themselves in a far, dark end of the chamber, that the quest was hard and wise, for that if she could ever weep she might also love. They had known her all her childhood; she had never sighed. Many men had she seen, suitors and courtiers, and had never turned her head after one went by. Her beauty was as still sunsets of bitter evenings when all the world is frore, a wonder and a chill. She was as a sun-stricken mountain uplifted alone, all beautiful with ice, a desolate and lonely radiance late at evening far up beyond the comfortable world, not quite to be companioned by the stars, the doom of the mountaineer.

If she could weep, they said, she could love, they said.

And she smiled pleasantly on those ardent princes, and troubadours concealing kingly names.

Then one by one they told, each suitor prince the story of his love, with outstretched hands and kneeling on the knee; and very sorry and pitiful were the tales, so that often up in the galleries some maid of the palace wept. And very graciously she nodded her head like a listless magnolia in the deeps of the night moving idly to all the breezes its glorious bloom.

And when the princes had told their desperate loves and had departed away with no other spoil than of their own tears only, even then there came the unknown troubadours and told their tales in song, concealing their gracious names.

And there was one, Ackronnion, clothed with rags, on which was the dust of roads, and underneath the rags was war-scarred armour whereon were dints of blows; and when he stroked his harp and sang his song, in the gallery above maidens wept, and even old lords chamberlain whimpered among themselves and thereafter laughed through their tears and said: "It is easy to make old people weep and to bring idle tears from lazy girls; but he will not set a-weeping the Queen of the Woods."

And graciously she nodded, and he was the last. And disconsolate went away those dukes and princes, and troubadours in disguise. Yet Ackronnion pondered as he went away.

King he was of Afarmah, Lool and Haf, over-lord of Zeroora and hilly Chang, and duke of the dukedoms of Molong and Mlash, none of them unfamiliar with romance or unknown or overlooked in the making of myth. He pondered as he went in his thin disguise.

Now by those that do not remember their childhood, having other things to do, be it understood that underneath fairyland, which is, as all men know, at the edge of the world, there dwelleth the Gladsome Beast. A synonym he for joy.

It is known how the lark in its zenith, children at play out-of-doors, good witches and jolly old parents have all been compared--how aptly!--with this very same Gladsome Beast. Only one "crab" he has (if I may use slang for a moment to make myself perfectly clear), only one drawback, and that is that in the gladness of his heart he spoils the cabbages of the Old Man Who Looks After Fairyland,--and of course he eats men.

It must further be understood that whoever may obtain the tears of the Glad-some Beast in a bowl, and become drunken upon them, may move all persons to shed tears of joy so long as he remains inspired by the potion to sing or to make music.

Now Ackronnion pondered in this wise: that if he could obtain the tears of the Gladsome Beast by means of his art, withholding him from violence by the spell of music, and if a friend should slay the Gladsome Beast before his weeping ceased-- for an end must come to weeping even with men--that so he might get safe away with the tears, and drink them before the Queen of the Woods and move her to tears of joy. He sought out therefore a humble knightly man who cared not for the beauty of Sylvia, Queen of the Woods, but had found a woodland maiden of his own once long ago in summer. And the man's name was Arrath, a subject of Ack-ronnion, a knight-at-arms of the spear-guard: and together they set out through the fields of fable until they came to Fairyland, a kingdom sunning itself (as all men know) for leagues along the edges of the world. And by a strange old pathway they came to the land they sought, through a wind blowing up the pathway sheer from space with a kind of metallic taste from the roving stars. Even so they came to the windy house of thatch where dwells the Old Man Who Looks After Fairyland sit-ting by parlour windows that look away from the world. He made them welcome in his star-ward parlour, telling them tales of Space, and when they named to him their perilous quest he said it would be a charity to kill the Gladsome Beast; for he was clearly one of these that liked not its happy ways. And then he took them out through his back door, for the front door had no pathway nor even a step--from it the old man used to empty his slops sheer on to the Southern Cross--and so they came to the garden wherein his cabbages were, and those flowers that only blow in Fairyland, turning their faces always towards the comet, and he pointed them out the way to the place he called Underneath, where the Gladsome Beast had his lair. Then they manoeuvered. Ackronnion was to go by the way of the steps with his harp and an agate bowl, while Arrath went round by a crag on the other side. Then the Old Man Who Looks After Fairyland went back to his windy house, mutter-ing angrily as he passed his cabbages, for he did not love the ways of the Gladsome Beast; and the two friends parted on their separate ways.

Nothing perceived them but that ominous crow glutted overlong already upon the flesh of man.

The wind blew bleak from the stars.

At first there was dangerous climbing, and then Ackronnion gained the smooth, broad steps that led from the edge to the lair, and at that moment heard at the top of the steps the continuous chuckles of the Gladsome Beast.

He feared then that its mirth might be insuperable, not to be saddened by the most grievous song; nevertheless he did not turn back then, but softly climbed the stairs and, placing the agate bowl upon a step, struck up the chaunt called Dolorous. It told of desolate, regretted things befallen happy cities long since in the prime of the world. It told of how the gods and beasts and men had long ago loved beautiful companions, and long ago in vain. It told of the golden host of happy hopes, but not of their achieving. It told how Love scorned Death, but told of Death's laughter. The contented chuckles of the Gladsome Beast suddenly ceased in his lair. He rose and shook himself. He was still unhappy. Ackronnion still sang on the chaunt called Dolorous. The Gladsome Beast came mournfully up to him. Ackronnion ceased not for the sake of his panic, but still sang on. He sang of the malignity of time. Two tears welled large in the eyes of the Gladsome Beast. Ackronnion moved the agate bowl to a suitable spot with his foot. He sang of autumn and of passing away. The the beast wept as the frore hills weep in the thaw, and the tears splashed big into the agate bowl. Ackronnion desperately chaunted on; he told of the glad unnoticed things men see and do not see again, of sunlight beheld unheeded on faces now withered away. The bowl was full. Ackronnion was desperate: the Beast was so close. Once he thought that its mouth was watering!--but it was only the tears that had run on the lips of the Beast. He felt as a morsel! The Beast was ceasing to weep! He sang of worlds that had disappointed the gods. And all of a sudden, crash! and the staunch spear of Arrath went home behind the shoulder, and the tears and the joyful ways of the Gladsome Beast were ended and over for ever.

And carefully they carried the bowl of tears away leaving the body of the Gladsome Beast as a change of diet for the ominous crow; and going by the windy house of thatch they said farewell to the Old Man Who Looks After Fairyland, who when he heard of the deed rubbed his hands together and mumbled again and again, "And a very good thing, too. My cabbages! My cabbages!"

And not long after Ackronnion sang again in the sylvan palace of the Queen of the Woods, having first drunk all the tears in his agate bowl. And it was a gala night, and all the court were there and ambassadors from the lands of legend and myth, and even some from Terra Cognita.

And Ackronnion sang as he never sang before, and will not sing again. O, but dolorous, dolorous, are all the ways of man, few and fierce are his days, and the end trouble, and vain, vain his endeavor: and woman--who shall tell of it?--her doom is written with man's by listless, careless gods with their faces to other spheres.

Somewhat thus he began, and then inspiration seized him, and all the trouble in the beauty of his song may not be set down by me: there was much of gladness in it, and all mingled with grief: it was like the way of man: it was like our destiny.

Sobs arose at his song, sighs came back along echoes: seneschals, soldiers, sobbed, and a clear cry made the maidens; like rain the tears came down from gallery to gallery.

All round the Queen of the Woods was a storm of sobbing and sorrow.

But no, she would not weep.

THE HOARD OF THE GIBBELINS

THE Gibbelins eat, as is well known, nothing less good than man. Their evil tower is joined to Terra Cognita, to the lands we know, by a bridge. Their hoard is beyond reason; avarice has no use for it; they have a separate cellar for emeralds and a separate cellar for sapphires; they have filled a hole with gold and dig it up when they need it. And the only use that is known for their ridiculous wealth is to attract to their larder a continual supply of food. In times of famine they have even been known to scatter rubies abroad, a little trail of them to some city of Man, and sure enough their larders would soon be full again.

Their tower stands on the other side of that river known to Homer--*ho rhoos okeanoio*, as he called it--which surrounds the world. And where the river is narrow and fordable the tower was built by the Gibbelins' gluttonous sires, for they liked to see burglars rowing easily to their steps. Some nourishment that common soil has not the huge trees drained there with their colossal roots from both banks of the river.

There the Gibbelins lived and discreditably fed. Alderic, Knight of the Order of the City and the Assault, hereditary Guardian of the King's Peace of Mind, a man not unremembered among makers of myth, pondered so long upon the Gibbelins' hoard that by now he deemed it his. Alas that I should say of so perilous a venture, undertaken at dead of night by a valourous man, that its motive was sheer avarice! Yet upon avarice only the Gibbelins relied to keep their larders full, and once in every hundred years sent spies into the cities of men to see how avarice did, and always the spies returned again to the tower saying that all was well.

It may be thought that, as the years went on and men came by fearful ends on that tower's wall, fewer and fewer would come to the Gibbelins' table: but the Gibbelins found otherwise.

Not in the folly and frivolity of his youth did Alderic come to the tower, but he studied carefully for several years the manner in which burglars met their doom when they went in search of the treasure that he considered his. *In every case they had entered by the door.*

He consulted those who gave advice on this quest; he noted every detail and cheerfully paid their fees, and determined to do nothing that they advised, for what were their clients now? No more than examples of the savoury art, and mere half-forgotten memories of a meal; and many, perhaps, no longer even that.

These were the requisites for the quest that these men used to advise: a horse, a boat, mail armour, and at least three men-at-arms. Some said, "Blow the horn at the tower door"; others said, "Do not touch it."

Alderic thus decided: he would take no horse down to the river's edge, he would not row along it in a boat, and he would go alone and by way of the Forest Unpassable.

How pass, you may say, the unpassable? This was his plan: there was a dragon he knew of who if peasants' prayers are heeded deserved to die, not alone because of the number of maidens he cruelly slew, but because he was bad for the crops; he ravaged the very land and was the bane of a dukedom.

Now Alderic determined to go up against him. So he took horse and spear and pricked till he met the dragon, and the dragon came out against him breathing bitter smoke. And to him Alderic shouted, "Hath foul dragon ever slain true knight?" And well the dragon knew that this had never been, and he hung his head and was silent, for he was glutted with blood. "Then," said the knight, "if thou would'st ever taste maiden's blood again thou shalt be my trusty steed, and if not, by this spear there shall befall thee all that the troubadours tell of the dooms of thy breed."

And the dragon did not open his ravening mouth, nor rush upon the knight, breathing out fire; for well he knew the fate of those that did these things, but he consented to the terms imposed, and swore to the knight to become his trusty steed.

It was on a saddle upon this dragon's back that Alderic afterwards sailed above the unpassable forest, even above the tops of those measureless trees, children of wonder. But first he pondered that subtle plan of his which was more profound than merely to avoid all that had been done before; and he commanded a blacksmith, and the blacksmith made him a pickaxe.

Now there was great rejoicing at the rumour of Alderic's quest, for all folk knew that he was a cautious man, and they deemed that he would succeed and enrich the world, and they rubbed their hands in the cities at the thought of largesse; and there was joy among all men in Alderic's country, except perchance among the lenders of money, who feared they would soon be paid. And there was rejoicing also because men hoped that when the Gibbelins were robbed of their hoard, they would shatter their high-built bridge and break the golden chains that bound them to the world, and drift back, they and their tower, to the moon, from which they had come and to which they rightly belonged. There was little love for the Gibbelins, though all men envied their hoard.

So they all cheered, that day when he mounted his dragon, as though he was already a conqueror, and what pleased them more than the good that they hoped he would do to the world was that he scattered gold as he rode away; for he would not need it, he said, if he found the Gibbelins' hoard, and he would not need it more if he smoked on the Gibbelins' table.

When they heard that he had rejected the advice of those that gave it, some said that the knight was mad, and others said he was greater than those what gave the advice, but none appreciated the worth of his plan.

He reasoned thus: for centuries men had been well advised and had gone by the cleverest way, while the Gibbelins came to expect them to come by boat and to look for them at the door whenever their larder was empty, even as a man looketh for a snipe in a marsh; but how, said Alderic, if a snipe should sit in the top of a tree, and would men find him there? Assuredly never! So Alderic decided to swim the river and not to go by the door, but to pick his way into the tower through the stone. Moreover, it was in his mind to work below the level of the ocean, the river (as Homer knew) that girdles the world, so that as soon as he made a hole in the wall the water should pour in, confounding the Gibbelins, and flooding the cellars, rumoured to be twenty feet in depth, and therein he would dive for emeralds as a diver dives for pearls.

And on the day that I tell of he galloped away from his home scattering largesse of gold, as I have said, and passed through many kingdoms, the dragon snapping at maidens as he went, but being unable to eat them because of the bit in his mouth, and earning no gentler reward than a spurthrust where he was softest. And so they came to the swart arboreal precipice of the unpassable forest. The dragon rose at it with a rattle of wings. Many a farmer near the edge of the worlds saw him up there where yet the twilight lingered, a faint, black, wavering line; and mistaking him for a row of geese going inland from the ocean, went into their houses cheerily rubbing their hands and saying that winter was coming, and that we should soon have snow. Soon even there the twilight faded away, and when they descended at the edge of the world it was night and the moon was shining. Ocean, the ancient river, narrow and shallow there, flowed by and made no murmur. Whether the Gibbelins banqueted or whether they watched by the door, they also made no murmur. And Alderic dismounted and took his armour off, and saying one prayer to his lady, swam with his pickaxe. He did not part from his sword, for fear that he meet with a Gibbelin. Landed the other side, he began to work at once, and all went well with him. Nothing put out its head from any window, and all were lighted so that nothing within could see him in the dark. The blows of his pickaxe were dulled in the deep walls. All night he worked, no sound came to molest him, and at dawn the last rock swerved and tumbled inwards, and the river poured in after. Then Alderic took a stone, and went to the bottom step, and hurled the stone at the door; he heard the echoes roll into the tower, then he ran back and dived through the hole in the wall.

He was in the emerald-cellar. There was no light in the lofty vault above him, but, diving through twenty feet of water, he felt the floor all rough with emeralds, and open coffers full of them. By a faint ray of the moon he saw that the water was green with them, and easily filling a satchel, he rose again to the surface; and there were the Gibbelins waist-deep in the water, with torches in their hands! And, without saying a word, *or even smiling*, they neatly hanged him on the outer wall--and the tale is one of those that have not a happy ending.

HOW NUTH WOULD HAVE PRACTISED HIS ART UPON THE GNOLES

DESPITE the advertisements of rival firms, it is probable that every trades-man knows that nobody in business at the present time has a position equal to that of Mr. Nuth. To those outside the magic circle of business, his name is scarcely known; he does not need to advertise, he is con-summate. He is superiour even to modern competition, and, whatever claims they boast, his rivals know it. His terms are moderate, so much cash down when when the goods are delivered, so much in blackmail afterwards. He consults your convenience. His skill may be counted upon; I have seen a shadow on a windy night move more noisily than Nuth, for Nuth is a burglar by trade. Men have been known to stay in country houses and to send a dealer afterwards to bargain for a piece of tap-estry that they saw there--some article of furniture, some picture. This is bad taste: but those whose culture is more elegant invariably send Nuth a night or two after their visit. He has a way with tapestry; you would scarcely notice that the edges had been cut. And often when I see some huge, new house full of old furniture and por-traits from other ages, I say to myself, "These mouldering chairs, these full-length ancestors and carved mahogany are the produce of the incomparable Nuth."

It may be urged against my use of the word incomparable that in the burglary business the name of Slith stands paramount and alone; and of this I am not igno-rant; but Slith is a classic, and lived long ago, and knew nothing at all of modern competition; besides which the surprising nature of his doom has possibly cast a glamour upon Slith that exaggerates in our eyes his undoubted merits.

It must not be thought that I am a friend of Nuth's; on the contrary such poli-tics as I have are on the side of Property; and he needs no words from me, for his position is almost unique in trade, being among the every few that do not need to advertise.

At the time that my story begins Nuth lived in a roomy house in Belgrave Square: in his inimitable way he had made friends with the caretaker. The place suited Nuth, and, whenever anyone came to inspect it before purchase, the caretaker used to praise the house in the words that Nuth had suggested. "If it wasn't for the drains," she would say, "it's the finest house in London," and when they pounced on this remark and asked questions about the drains, she would answer them that the drains also were good, but not so good as the house. They did not see Nuth when they went over the rooms, but Nuth was there.

Here in a neat black dress on one spring morning came an old woman whose bonnet was lined with red, asking for Mr. Nuth; and with her came her large and awkward son. Mrs. Eggins, the caretaker, glanced up the street, and then she let them in, and left them to wait in the drawing-room amongst furniture all mysterious with sheets. For a long while they waited, and then there was a smell of pipe-tobacco, and there was Nuth standing quite close to them.

"Lord," said the old woman whose bonnet was lined with red, "you did make me start." And then she saw by his eyes that that was not the way to speak to Mr. Nuth.

And at last Nuth spoke, and very nervously the old woman explained that her son was a likely lad, and had been in business already but wanted to better himself, and she wanted Mr. Nuth to teach him a livelihood.

First of all Nuth wanted to see a business reference, and when he was shown one from a jeweller with whom he happened to be hand-in-glove the upshot of it was that he agreed to take young Tonker (for this was the surname of the likely lad) and to make him his apprentice. And the old woman whose bonnet was lined with red went back to her little cottage in the country, and every evening said to her old man, "Tonker, we must fasten the shutters of a night-time, for Tommy's a burglar now."

The details of the likely lad's apprenticeship I do not propose to give; for those that are in the business know those details already, and those that are in other businesses care only for their own, while men of leisure who have no trade at all would fail to appreciate the gradual degrees by which Tommy Tonker came first to cross bare boards, covered with little obstacles in the dark, without making any sound, and then to go silently up creaky stairs, and then to open doors, and lastly to climb.

Let it suffice that the business prospered greatly, while glowing reports of Tommy Tonker's progress were sent from time to time to the old woman whose bonnet was lined with red in the labourious handwriting of Nuth. Nuth had given up lessons in writing very early, for he seemed to have some prejudice against forgery, and therefore considered writing a waste of time. And then there came the transaction with Lord Castlenorman at his Surrey residence. Nuth selected a Saturday night, for it chanced that Saturday was observed as Sabbath in the family of Lord Castlenorman, and by eleven o'clock the whole house was quiet. Five minutes before midnight Tommy Tonker, instructed by Mr. Nuth, who waited outside, came away with one pocketful of rings and shirt-studs. It was quite a light pocketful, but the jewellers in Paris could not match it without sending specially to Africa, so that Lord Castlenorman had to borrow bone shirt-studs.

Not even rumour whispered the name of Nuth. Were I to say that this turned his head, there are those to whom the assertion would give pain, for his associates hold that his astute judgment was unaffected by circumstance. I will say, therefore, that it spurred his genius to plan what no burglar had ever planned before. It was nothing less than to burgle the house of the gnoles. And this that abstemious man unfolded to Tonker over a cup of tea. Had Tonker not been nearly insane with pride over their recent transaction, and had he not been blinded by a veneration for Nuth, he would have--but I cry over spilt milk. He expostulated respectfully; he said he would rather not go; he said it was not fair; he allowed himself to argue; and in the end, one windy October morning with a menace in the air found him and Nuth drawing near to the dreadful wood.

Nuth, by weighing little emeralds against pieces of common rock, had ascertained the probable weight of those house-ornaments that the gnoles are believed to possess in the narrow, lofty house wherein they have dwelt from of old. They decided to steal two emeralds and to carry them between them on a cloak; but if they should be too heavy one must be dropped at once. Nuth warned young Tonker against greed, and explained that the emeralds were worth less than cheese until they were safe away from the dreadful wood.

Everything had been planned, and they walked now in silence.

No track led up to the sinister gloom of the trees, either of men or cattle; not even a poacher had been there snaring elves for over a hundred years. You did not trespass twice in the dells of the gnoles. And, apart from the things that were done there, the trees themselves were a warning, and did not wear the wholesome look of those that we plant ourselves.

The nearest village was some miles away with the backs of all its houses turned to the wood, and without one window at all facing in that direction. They did not speak of it there, and elsewhere it is unheard of.

Into this wood stepped Nuth and Tommy Tonker. They had no firearms. Tonker had asked for a pistol, but Nuth replied that the sound of a shot "would bring everything down on us," and no more was said about it.

Into the wood they went all day, deeper and deeper. They saw the skeleton of some early Georgian poacher nailed to a door in an oak tree; sometimes they saw a fairy scuttle away from them; once Tonker stepped heavily on a hard, dry stick, after which they both lay still for twenty minutes. And the sunset flared full of omens through the tree trunks, and night fell, and they came by fitful starlight, as Nuth had foreseen, to that lean, high house where the gnoles so secretly dwelt.

All was so silent by that unvalued house that the faded courage of Tonker flickered up, but to Nuth's experienced sense it seemed too silent; and all the while there was that look in the sky that was worse than a spoken doom, so that Nuth, as is often the case when men are in doubt, had leisure to fear the worst. Nevertheless he did not abandon the business, but sent the likely lad with the instruments of his trade by means of the ladder to the old green casement. And the moment that Tonker touched the withered boards, the silence that, though ominous, was earthly, became unearthly like the touch of a ghoul. And Tonker heard his breath offending against that silence, and his heart was like mad drums in a night attack, and a string of one of his sandals went tap on a rung of a ladder, and the leaves of the forest were mute, and the breeze of the night was still; and Tonker prayed that a mouse or a mole might make any noise at all, but not a creature stirred, even Nuth was still. And then and there, while yet he was undiscovered, the likely lad made up his mind, as he should have done long before, to leave those colossal emeralds where they were and have nothing further to do with the lean, high house of the gnoles, but to quit this sinister wood in the nick of time and retire from business at once and buy a place in the country. Then he descended softly and beckoned to Nuth. But the gnoles had watched him though knavish holes that they bore in trunks of the trees, and the unearthly silence gave way, as it were with a grace, to the rapid screams of Tonker as they picked him up from behind--screams that came faster and faster until they were incoherent. And where they took him it is not good to ask, and what they did with him I shall not say.

Nuth looked on for a while from the corner of the house with a mild surprise on his face as he rubbed his chin, for the trick of the holes in the trees was new to him; then he stole nimbly away through the dreadful wood.

"And did they catch Nuth?" you ask me, gentle reader.

"Oh, no, my child" (for such a question is childish). "Nobody ever catches Nuth."

HOW ONE CAME, AS WAS FORETOLD, TO THE CITY OF NEVER

THE child that played about the terraces and gardens in sight of the Surrey hills never knew that it was he that should come to the Ultimate City, never knew that he should see the Under Pits, the barbicans and the holy minarets of the mightiest city known. I think of him now as a child with a little red watering-can going about the gardens on a summer's day that lit the warm south country, his imagination delighted with all tales of quite little adventures, and all the while there was reserved for him that feat at which men wonder.

Looking in other directions, away from the Surrey hills, through all his infancy he saw that precipice that, wall above wall and mountain above mountain, stands at the edge of the World, and in perpetual twilight alone with the Moon and the Sun holds up the inconceivable City of Never. To read its streets he was destined; prophecy knew it. He had the magic halter, and a worn old rope it was; an old wayfaring woman had given it to him: it had the power to hold any animal whose race had never known captivity, such as the unicorn, the hippogriff Pegasus, dragons and wyverns; but with a lion, giraffe, camel or horse, it was useless.

How often we have seen that City of Never, that marvel of the Nations! Not when it is night in the World, and we can see no further than the stars; not when the sun is shining where we dwell, dazzling our eyes; but when the sun has set on some stormy days, all at once repentant at evening, and those glittering cliffs reveal themselves which we almost take to be clouds, and it is twilight with us as it is for ever with them, then on their gleaming summits we see those golden domes that overpeer the edges of the World and seem to dance with dignity and calm in that gentle light of evening that is Wonder's native haunt. Then does the City of Never, unvisited and afar, look long at her sister the World.

It had been prophecied that he should come there. They knew it when the pebbles were being made and before the isles of coral were given unto the sea. And thus the prophecy came unto fulfilment and passed into history, and so at length to Oblivion, out of which I drag it as it goes floating by, into which I shall one day tumble. The hippogriffs dance before dawn in the upper air; long before sunrise flashes upon our lawns they go to glitter in light that has not yet come to the World, and as the dawn works up from the ragged hills and the stars feel it they go slanting earthwards, till sunlight touches the tops of the tallest trees, and the hippogriffs alight with a rattle of quills and fold their wings and gallop and gambol away till they come to some prosperous, wealthy, detestable town, and they leap at once from the fields and soar away from the sight of it, pursued by the horrible smoke of it until they come again to the pure blue air.

He whom prophecy had named from of old to come to the City of Never, went down one midnight with his magic halter to a lake-side where the hippogriffs alighted at dawn, for the turf was soft there and they could gallop far before they came to a town, and there he waited hidden near their hoofmarks. And the stars paled a little and grew indistinct; but there was no other sign as yet of the dawn, when there appeared far up in the deeps of the night two little saffron specks, then four and five: it was the hippogriffs dancing and twirling around in the sun. Another flock joined them, there were twelve of them now; they danced there, flashing their colours back to the sun, they descended in wide curves slowly; trees down on earth revealed against the sky, jet-black each delicate twig; a star disappeared from a cluster, now another; and dawn came on like music, like a new song. Ducks shot by to the lake from still dark fields of corn, far voices uttered, a colour grew upon water, and still the hippogriffs gloried in the light, revelling up in the sky; but when pigeons stirred on the branches and the first small bird was abroad, and little coots from the rushes ventured to peer about, then there came down on a sudden with a thunder of feathers the hippogriffs, and, as they landed from their celestial heights all bathed with the day's first sunlight, the man whose destiny it was as from of old to come to the City of Never, sprang up and caught the last with the magic halter. It plunged, but could not escape it, for the hippogriffs are of the uncaptured races, and magic has power over the magical, so the man mounted it, and it soared again for the heights whence it had come, as a wounded beast goes home. But when they came to the heights that venturous rider saw huge and fair to the left of him the destined City of Never, and he beheld the towers of Lel and Lek, Neerid and Akathooma, and the cliffs of Toldenarba a-glistening in the twilight like an alabaster statue of the Evening. Towards them he wrenched the halter, towards Toldenarba and the Under Pits; the wings of the hippogriff roared as the halter turned him. Of the Under Pits who shall tell? Their mystery is secret. It is held by some that they are the sources of night, and that darkness pours from them at evening upon the world; while others hint that knowledge of these might undo our civilization.

There watched him ceaselessly from the Under Pits those eyes whose duty it is; from further within and deeper, the bats what dwell there arose when they saw the surprise in the eyes; the sentinels on the bulwarks beheld that stream of bats and lifted up their spears as it were for war. Nevertheless when they perceived that that war for which they watched was not now come upon them, they lowered their spears and suffered him to enter, and he passed whirring through the earthward gateway. Even so he came, as foretold, to the City of Never perched upon Toldenarba, and saw late twilight on those pinnacles that know no other light. All the domes were of copper, but the spires on their summits were gold. Little steps of onyx ran all this way and that. With cobbled agates were its streets a glory. Through small square panes of rose-quartz the citizens looked from their houses. To them as they looked abroad the World far-off seemed happy. Clad though that city was in one robe always, in twilight, yet was its beauty worthy of even so lovely a wonder: city and twilight were both peerless but for each other. Built of a stone unknown in the world we tread were its bastions, quarried we known not where, but called by the gnomes *abyx*, it so flashed back to the twilight its glories, colour for colour, that none can say of them where their boundary is, and which the eternal twilight, and which the City of Never; they are the twin-born children, the fairest daughters of Wonder. Time had been there, but not to the domes that were made of copper, the rest he had left untouched, even he, the destroyer of cities, by what bribe I know not averted. Nevertheless they often wept in Never for change and passing away, mourning catastrophes in other worlds, and they built temples sometimes to ruined stars that had fallen flaming down from the Milky Way, giving them worship still when by us long since forgotten. Other temples they have--who knows to what divinities?

And he that was destined alone of men to come to the City of Never was well content to behold it as he trotted down its agate street, with the wings of his hippogriff furled, seeing at either side of him marvel on marvel of which even China is ignorant. Then as he neared the city's further rampart by which no inhabitant stirred, and looked in a direction to which no houses faced with any rose-pink windows, he suddenly saw far-off, dwarfing the mountains, an even greater city. Whether that city was built upon the twilight or whether it rose from the coasts of some other world he did not know. He saw it dominate the City of Never, and strove to reach it; but at this unmeasured home of unknown colossi the hippogriff shied frantically, and neither the magic halter nor anything that he did could make the monster face it. At last, from the City of Never's lonely outskirts where no inhabitants walked, the rider turned slowly earthward. He knew now why all the windows faced this way--the denizens of the twilight gazed at the world and not at a greater than them. Then from the last step of the earthward stairway, like lead past the Under Pits and down the glittering face of Toldenarba, down from the overshadowed glories of the gold-tipped City of Never and out of perpetual twilight, swooped the man on his winged monster: the wind that slept at the time leaped up like a dog at their onrush, it uttered a cry and ran past them. Down on the World it was morning; night was roaming away with his cloak trailed behind him, with mists turned over and over as he went, the orb was grey but it glittered, lights blinked surprisingly in early windows, forth over wet, dim fields went cows from their houses: even in this hour touched the fields again the feet of the hippogriff. And the moment that the man dismounted and took off his magic halter the hippogriff flew slanting away with a whirr, going back to some airy dancing-place of his people.

And he that surmounted glittering Toldenarba and came alone of men to the City of Never has his name and his fame among nations; but he and the people of that twilit city well know two things unguessed by other men, they that there is another city fairer than theirs, and he--a deed unaccomplished.

THE CORONATION OF MR. THOMAS SHAP

I T was the occupation of Mr. Thomas Shap to persuade customers that the goods were genuine and of an excellent quality, and that as regards the price their unspoken will was consulted. And in order to carry on this occupation he went by train very early every morning some few miles nearer to the City from the suburb in which he slept. This was the use to which he put his life.

From the moment when he first perceived (not as one reads a thing in a book, but as truths are revealed to one's instinct) the very beastliness of his occupation, and of the house that he slept in, its shape, make and pretensions, and even the clothes that he wore; from that moment he withdrew his dreams from it, his fancies, his ambitions, everything in fact except that ponderable Mr. Shap that dressed in a frock-coat, bought tickets and handled money and could in turn be handled by the statistician. The priest's share in Mr. Shap, the share of the poet, never caught the early train to the City at all.

He used to take little flights of fancy at first, dwelt all day in his dreamy way on fields and rivers lying in the sunlight where it strikes the world more brilliantly further South. And then he began to imagine butterflies there; after that, silken people and the temples they built to their gods.

They noticed that he was silent, and even absent at times, but they found no fault with his behaviour with customers, to whom he remained as plausible as of old. So he dreamed for a year, and his fancy gained strength as he dreamed. He still read halfpenny papers in the train, still discussed the passing day's ephemeral topic, still voted at elections, though he no longer did these things with the whole Shap--his soul was no longer in them.

He had had a pleasant year, his imagination was all new to him still, and it had often discovered beautiful things away where it went, southeast at the edge of the twilight. And he had a matter-of-fact and logical mind, so that he often said, "Why should I pay my twopence at the electric theatre when I can see all sorts of things quite easily without?" Whatever he did was logical before anything else, and those that knew him always spoke of Shap as "a sound, sane, level-headed man."

On far the most important day of his life he went as usual to town by the early train to sell plausible articles to customers, while the spiritual Shap roamed off to fanciful lands. As he walked from the station, dreamy but wide awake, it suddenly struck him that the real Shap was not the one walking to Business in black and ugly clothes, but he who roamed along a jungle's edge near the ramparts of an old and Eastern city that rose up sheer from the sand, and against which the desert lapped with one eternal wave. He used to fancy the name of that city was Larkar. "After all, the fancy is as real as the body," he said with perfect logic. It was a dangerous theory.

For that other life that he led he realized, as in Business, the importance and value of method. He did not let his fancy roam too far until it perfectly knew its first surroundings. Particularly he avoided the jungle--he was not afraid to meet a tiger there (after all it was not real), but stranger things might crouch there. Slowly he built up Larkar: rampart by rampart, towers for archers, gateway of brass, and all. And then one day he argued, and quite rightly, that all the silk-clad people in its streets, their camels, their wares that come from Inkustahn, the city itself, were all the things of his will--and then he made himself King. He smiled after that when people did not raise their hats to him in the street, as he walked from the station to Business; but he was sufficiently practical for recognize that it was better not to talk of this to those that only knew him as Mr. Shap.

Now that he was King in the city of Larkar and in all the desert that lay to the East and North he sent his fancy to wander further afield. He took the regiments of his camel-guard and went jingling out of Larkar, with little silver bells under the camels' chins, and came to other cities far-off on the yellow sand, with clear white walls and towers, uplifting themselves in the sun. Through their gates he passed with his three silken regiments, the light-blue regiment of the camel-guards being upon his right and the green regiment riding at his left, the lilac regiment going on before. When he had gone through the streets of any city and observed the ways of its people, and had seen the way that the sunlight struck its towers, he would pro-claim himself King there, and then ride on in fancy. So he passed from city to city and from land to land. Clear-sighted though Mr. Shap was, I think he overlooked the lust of aggrandizement to which kings have so often been victims; and so it was that when the first few cities had opened their gleaming gates and he saw peoples prostrate before his camel, and spearmen cheering along countless balconies, and priests come out to do him reverence, he that had never had even the lowliest authority in the familiar world became unwisely insatiate. He let his fancy ride at inordinate speed, he forsook method, scarce was he king of a land but he yearned to extend his borders; so he journeyed deeper and deeper into the wholly unknown. The concentration that he gave to this inordinate progress through countries of which history is ignorant and cities so fantastic in their bulwarks that, though their inhabitants were human, yet the foe that they feared seemed something less or more; the amazement with which he beheld gates and towers unknown even to art, and furtive people thronging intricate ways to acclaim him as their sovereign--all these things began to affect his capacity for Business. He knew as well as any that his fancy could not rule these beautiful lands unless that other Shap, however unimportant, were well sheltered and fed: and shelter and food meant money, and money, Business. His was more like the mistake of some gambler with cunning schemes who overlooks human greed. One day his fancy, riding in the morning, came to a city gorgeous as the sunrise, in whose opalescent wall were gates of gold, so huge that a river poured between the bars, floating in, when the gates were opened, large galleons under sail. Thence there came dancing out a company with instruments, and made a melody all around the wall; that morning Mr. Shap, the bodily Shap in London, forgot the train to town.

Until a year ago he had never imagined at all; it is not to be wondered at that all these things now newly seen by his fancy should play tricks at first with the memory of even so sane a man. He gave up reading the papers altogether, he lost all interest in politics, he cared less and less for things that were going on around him. This unfortunate missing of the morning train even occurred again, and the firm spoke to him severely about it. But he had his consolation. Were not Arathrion and Argun Zeerith and all the level coasts of Oora his? And even as the firm found fault with him his fancy watched the yaks on weary journeys, slow specks against the snow-fields, bringing tribute; and saw the green eyes of the mountain men who had looked at him strangely in the city of Nith when he had entered it by the desert door. Yet his logic did not forsake him; he knew well that his strange subjects did not exist, but he was prouder of having created them with his brain, than merely of ruling them only; thus in his pride he felt himself something more great than a king, he did not dare to think what! He went into the temple of the city of Zorra and stood some time there alone: all the priests kneeled to him when he came away.

He cared less and less for the things we care about, for the affairs of Shap, the business-man in London. He began to despise the man with a royal contempt.

One day when he sat in Sowla, the city of the Thuls, throned on one amethyst, he decided, and it was proclaimed on the moment by silver trumpets all along the land, that he would be crowned as king over all the lands of Wonder.

By that old temple where the Thuls worshipped, year in, year out, for over a thousand years, they pitched pavilions in the open air. The trees that blew there threw out radiant scents unknown in any countries that know the map; the stars blazed fiercely for that famous occasion. A fountain hurled up, clattering, ceaselessly into the air armfuls on armfuls of diamonds. A deep hush waited for the golden trumpets, the holy coronation night was come. At the top of those old, worn steps, going down we know not whither, stood the king in the emerald-and-amethyst cloak, the ancient garb of the Thuls; beside him lay that Sphinx that for the last few weeks had advised him in his affairs.

Slowly, with music when the trumpets sounded, came up towards him from we know not where, one-hundred-and-twenty archbishops, twenty angels and two archangels, with that terrific crown, the diadem of the Thuls. They knew as they came up to him that promotion awaited them all because of this night's work. Silent, majestic, the king awaited them.

The doctors downstairs were sitting over their supper, the warders softly slipped from room to room, and when in that cosy dormitory of Hanwell they saw the king still standing erect and royal, his face resolute, they came up to him and addressed him:

"Go to bed," they said--"pretty bed." So he lay down and soon was fast asleep: the great day was over.

CHU-BU AND SHEEMISH

IT was the custom on Tuesdays in the temple of Chu-bu for the priests to enter at evening and chant, "There is none but Chu-bu."

And all the people rejoiced and cried out, "There is none but Chu-bu." And honey was offered to Chu-bu, and maize and fat. Thus was he magnified.

Chu-bu was an idol of some antiquity, as may be seen from the colour of the wood. He had been carved out of mahogany, and after he was carved he had been polished. Then they had set him up on the diorite pedestal with the brazier in front of it for burning spices and the flat gold plates for fat. Thus they worshipped Chu-bu.

He must have been there for over a hundred years when one day the priests came in with another idol into the temple of Chu-bu and set it up on a pedestal near Chu-bu's and sang, "There is also Sheemish."

And all the people rejoiced and cried out, "There is also Sheemish."

Sheemish was palpably a modern idol, and although the wood was stained with a dark-red dye, you could see that he had only just been carved. And honey was offered to Sheemish as well as Chu-bu, and also maize and fat.

The fury of Chu-bu knew no time-limit: he was furious all that night, and next day he was furious still. The situation called for immediate miracles. To devastate the city with a pestilence and kill all his priests was scarcely within his power, therefore he wisely concentrated such divine powers as he had in commanding a little earthquake. "Thus," thought Chu-bu, "will I reassert myself as the only god, and men shall spit upon Sheemish."

Chu-bu willed it and willed it and still no earthquake came, when suddenly he was aware that the hated Sheemish was daring to attempt a miracle too. He ceased to busy himself about the earthquake and listened, or shall I say felt, for what Sheemish was thinking; for gods are aware of what passes in the mind by a sense that is other than any of our five. Sheemish was trying to make an earthquake too.

The new god's motive was probably to assert himself. I doubt if Chu-bu understood or cared for his motive; it was sufficient for an idol already aflame with jealousy that his detestable rival was on the verge of a miracle. All the power of Chu-bu veered round at once and set dead against an earthquake, even a little one. It was thus in the temple of Chu-bu for some time, and then no earthquake came.

To be a god and to fail to achieve a miracle is a despairing sensation; it is as though among men one should determine upon a hearty sneeze and as though no sneeze should come; it is as though one should try to swim in heavy boots or remember a name that is utterly forgotten: all these pains were Sheemish's.

And upon Tuesday the priests came in, and the people, and they did worship Chu-bu and offered fat to him, saying, "O Chu-bu who made everything," and then the priests sang, "There is also Sheemish"; and Chu-bu was put to shame and spake not for three days.

Now there were holy birds in the temple of Chu-bu, and when the third day was come and the night thereof, it was as it were revealed to the mind of Chu-bu, that there was dirt upon the head of Sheemish.

And Chu-bu spake unto Sheemish as speak the gods, moving no lips nor yet disturbing the silence, saying, "There is dirt upon thy head, O Sheemish." All night long he muttered again and again, "there is dirt upon Sheemish's head." And when it was dawn and voices were heard far off, Chu-bu became exultant with Earth's awakening things, and cried out till the sun was high, "Dirt, dirt, dirt, upon the head of Sheemish," and at noon he said, "So Sheemish would be a god." Thus was Sheemish confounded.

And with Tuesday one came and washed his head with rose-water, and he was worshipped again when they sang "There is also Sheemish." And yet was Chu-bu content, for he said, "The head of Sheemish has been defiled," and again, "His head was defiled, it is enough." And one evening lo! there was dirt on the head of Chu-bu also, and the thing was perceived of Sheemish.

It is not with the gods as it is with men. We are angry one with another and turn from our anger again, but the wrath of the gods is enduring. Chu-bu remembered and Sheemish did not forget. They spake as we do not speak, in silence yet heard of each other, nor were their thoughts as our thoughts. We should not judge them merely by human standards. All night long they spake and all night said these words only: "Dirty Chu-bu," "Dirty Sheemish." "Dirty Chu-bu," "Dirty Sheemish," all night long. Their wrath had not tired at dawn, and neither had wearied of his accusation. And gradually Chu-bu came to realize that he was nothing more than the equal of Sheemish. All gods are jealous, but this equality with the upstart Sheemish, a thing of painted wood a hundred years newer than Chu-bu, and this worship given to Sheemish in Chu-bu's own temple, were particularly bitter. Chu-bu was jealous even for a god; and when Tuesday came again, the third day of Sheemish's worship, Chu-bu could bear it no longer. He felt that his anger must be revealed at all costs, and he returned with all the vehemence of his will to achieving a little earthquake. The worshippers had just gone from his temple when Chu-bu settled his will to attain this miracle. Now and then his meditations were disturbed by that now familiar dictum, "Dirty Chu-bu," but Chu-bu willed ferociously, not even stopping to say what he longed to say and had already said nine hundred times, and presently even these interruptions ceased.

They ceased because Sheemish had returned to a project that he had never definitely abandoned, the desire to assert himself and exalt himself over Chu-bu by performing a miracle, and the district being volcanic he had chosen a little earthquake as the miracle most easily accomplished by a small god.

Now an earthquake that is commanded by two gods has double the chance of fulfilment than when it is willed by one, and an incalculably greater chance than when two gods are pulling different ways; as, to take the case of older and greater gods, when the sun and the moon pull in the same direction we have the biggest tides.

Chu-bu knew nothing of the theory of tides, and was too much occupied with his miracle to notice what Sheemish was doing. And suddenly the miracle was an accomplished thing.

It was a very local earthquake, for there are other gods than Chu-bu or even Sheemish, and it was only a little one as the gods had willed, but it loosened some monoliths in a colonnade that supported one side of the temple and the whole of one wall fell in, and the low huts of the people of that city were shaken a little and some of their doors were jammed so that they would not open; it was enough, and for a moment it seemed that it was all; neither Chu-bu nor Sheemish commanded there should be more, but they had set in motion an old law older than Chu-bu, the law of gravity that that colonnade had held back for a hundred years, and the temple of Chu-bu quivered and then stood still, swayed once and was overthrown, on the heads of Chu-bu and Sheemish.

No one rebuilt it, for nobody dared to near such terrible gods. Some said that Chu-bu wrought the miracle, but some said Sheemish, and thereof schism was born. The weakly amiable, alarmed by the bitterness of rival sects, sought compromise and said that both had wrought it, but no one guessed the truth that the thing was done in rivalry.

And a saying arose, and both sects held this belief in common, that whoso toucheth Chu-bu shall die or whoso looketh upon Sheemish.

That is how Chu-bu came into my possession when I travelled once beyond the hills of Ting. I found him in the fallen temple of Chu-bu with his hands and toes sticking up out of the rubbish, lying upon his back, and in that attitude just as I found him I keep him to this day on my mantlepiece, as he is less liable to be upset that way. Sheemish was broken, so I left him where he was.

And there is something so helpless about Chu-bu with his fat hands stuck up in the air that sometimes I am moved out of compassion to bow down to him and pray, saying, "O Chu-bu, thou that made everything, help thy servant."

Chu-bu cannot do much, though once I am sure that at a game of bridge he sent me the ace of trumps after I had not held a card worth having for the whole of the evening. And chance alone could have done as much as that for me. But I do not tell this to Chu-bu.

THE WONDERFUL WINDOW

THE old man in the Oriental-looking robe was being moved on by the police, and it was this that attracted to him and the parcel under his arm the attention of Mr. Sladden, whose livelihood was earned in the emporium of Messrs. Mergin and Chater, that is to say in their establishment.

Mr. Sladden had the reputation of being the silliest young man in Business; a touch of romance--a mere suggestion of it--would send his eyes gazing away as though the walls of the emporium were of gossamer and London itself a myth, instead of attending to customers.

Merely the fact that the dirty piece of paper that wrapped the old man's parcel was covered with Arabic writing was enough to give Mr. Sladden the ideas of romance, and he followed until the little crowd fell off and the stranger stopped by the kerb and unwrapped his parcel and prepared to sell the thing that was inside it. It was a little window in old wood with small panes set in lead; it was not much more than a foot in breadth and was under two feet long. Mr. Sladden had never before seen a window sold in the street, so he asked the price of it.

"Its price is all you possess," said the old man.

"Where did you get it?" said Mr. Sladden, for it was a strange window.

"I gave all that I possessed for it in the streets of Baghdad."

"Did you possess much?" said Mr. Sladden.

"I had all that I wanted," he said, "except this window."

"It must be a good window," said the young man.

"It is a magical window," said the old one.

"I have only ten shillings on me, but I have fifteen-and-six at home."

The old man thought for a while.

"Then twenty-five-and-sixpence is the price of the window," he said.

It was only when the bargain was completed and the ten shillings paid and the strange old man was coming for his fifteen-and-six and to fit the magical window into his only room that it occurred to Mr. Sladden's mind that he did not want a window. And then they were at the door of the house in which he rented a room, and it seemed too late to explain.

The stranger demanded privacy when he fitted up the window, so Mr. Sladden remained outside the door at the top of a little flight of creaky stairs. He heard no sound of hammering.

And presently the strange old man came out with his faded yellow robe and his great beard, and his eyes on far-off places. "It is finished," he said, and he and the young man parted. And whether he remained a spot of colour and an anachronism in London, or whether he ever came again to Baghdad, and what dark hands kept on the circulation of his twenty-five-and-six, Mr. Sladden never knew.

Mr. Sladden entered the bare-boarded room in which he slept and spent all his indoor hours between closing-time and the hour at which Messrs. Mergin and Chater commenced. To the Penates of so dingy a room his neat frock-coat must have been a continual wonder. Mr. Sladden took it off and folded it carefully; and there was the old man's window rather high up in the wall. There had been no window in that wall hitherto, nor any ornament at all but a small cupboard, so when Mr. Sladden had put his frock-coat safely away he glanced through his new window. It was where his cupboard had been in which he kept his tea-things: they were all standing on the table now. When Mr. Sladden glanced through his new window it was late in a summer's evening; the butterflies some while ago would have closed their wings, though the bat would scarcely yet be drifting abroad--but this was in London: the shops were shut and street-lamps not yet lighted.

Mr. Sladden rubbed his eyes, then rubbed the window, and still he saw a sky of blazing blue, and far, far down beneath him, so that no sound came up from it or smoke of chimneys, a mediaeval city set with towers; brown roofs and cobbled streets, and then white walls and buttresses, and beyond them bright green fields and tiny streams. On the towers archers lolled, and along the walls were pikemen, and now and then a wagon went down some old-world street and lumbered through the gateway and out to the country, and now and then a wagon drew up to the city from the mist that was rolling with evening over the fields. Sometimes folks put their heads out of lattice windows, sometimes some idle troubadour seemed to sing, and nobody hurried or troubled about anything. Airy and dizzy though the distance was, for Mr. Sladden seemed higher above the city than any cathedral gargoyle, yet one clear detail he obtained as a clue: the banners floating from every tower over the idle archers had little golden dragons all over a pure white field.

He heard motor-buses roar by his other window, he heard the newsboys howling.

Mr. Sladden grew dreamier than ever after that on the premises, in the establishment of Messrs. Mergin and Chater. But in one matter he was wise and wakeful: he made continuous and careful inquiries about the golden dragons on a white flag, and talked to no one of his wonderful window. He came to know the flags of every king in Europe, he even dabbled in history, he made inquiries at shops that understood heraldry, but nowhere could he learn any trace of little dragons *or on a field argent*. And when it seemed that for him alone those golden dragons had fluttered he came to love them as an exile in some desert might love the lilies of his home or as a sick man might love swallows when he cannot easily live to another spring.

As soon as Messrs. Mergin and Chater closed, Mr. Sladden used to go back to his dingy room and gaze though the wonderful window until it grew dark in the city and the guard would go with a lantern round the ramparts and the night came up like velvet, full of strange stars. Another clue he tried to obtain one night by jotting down the shapes of the constellations, but this led him no further, for they were unlike any that shone upon either hemisphere.

Each day as soon as he woke he went first to the wonderful window, and there was the city, diminutive in the distance, all shining in the morning, and the golden dragons dancing in the sun, and the archers stretching themselves or swinging their arms on the tops of the windy towers. The window would not open, so that he never heard the songs that the troubadours sang down there beneath the gilded balconies; he did not even hear the belfries' chimes, though he saw the jackdaws routed every hour from their homes. And the first thing that he always did was to cast his eye round all the little towers that rose up from the ramparts to see that the little golden dragons were flying there on their flags. And when he saw them flaunting themselves on white folds from every tower against the marvelous deep blue of the sky he dressed contentedly, and, taking one last look, went off to his work with a glory in his mind. It would have been difficult for the customers of Messrs. Mergin and Chater to guess the precise ambition of Mr. Sladden as he walked before them in his neat frock-coat: it was that he might be a man-at-arms or an archer in order to fight for the little golden dragons that flew on a white flag for an unknown king in an inaccessible city. At first Mr. Sladden used to walk round and round the mean street that he lived in, but he gained no clue from that; and soon he noticed that quite different winds blew below his wonderful window from those that blew on the other side of the house.

In August the evenings began to grow shorter: this was the very remark that the other employees made to him at the emporium, so that he almost feared that they suspected his secret, and he had much less time for the wonderful window, for lights were few down there and they blinked out early.

One morning late in August, just before he went to Business, Mr. Sladden saw a company of pikemen running down the cobbled road towards the gateway of the mediaeval city--Golden Dragon City he used to call it alone in his own mind, but he never spoke of it to anyone. The next thing that he noticed was that the archers were handling round bundles of arrows in addition to the quivers which they wore. Heads were thrust out of windows more than usual, a woman ran out and called some children indoors, a knight rode down the street, and then more pikemen appeared along the walls, and all the jack-daws were in the air. In the street no troubadour sang. Mr. Sladden took one look along the towers to see that the flags were flying, and all the golden dragons were streaming in the wind. Then he had to go to Business. He took a bus back that evening and ran upstairs. Nothing seemed to be happening in Golden Dragon City except a crowd in the cobbled street that led down to the gateway; the archers seemed to be reclining as usual lazily in their towers, and then a white flag went down with all its golden dragons; he did not see at first that all the archers were dead. The crowd was pouring towards him, towards the precipitous wall from which he looked; men with a white flag covered with golden dragons were moving backwards slowly, men with another flag were pressing them, a flag on which there was one huge red bear. Another banner went down upon a tower. Then he saw it all: the golden dragons were being beaten--his little golden dragons. The men of the bear were coming under the window; what ever he threw from that height would fall with terrific force: fire-irons, coal, his clock, whatever he had--he would fight for his little golden dragons yet. A flame broke out from one of the towers and licked the feet of a reclining archer; he did not stir. And now the alien standard was out of sight directly underneath. Mr. Sladden broke the panes of the wonderful window and wrenched away with a poker the lead that held them. Just as the glass broke he saw a banner covered with golden dragons fluttering still, and then as he drew back to hurl the poker there came to him the scent of mysterious spices, and there was nothing there, not even the daylight, for behind the fragments of the wonderful window was nothing but that small cupboard in which he kept his tea-things.

And though Mr. Sladden is older now and knows more of the world, and even has a Business of his own, he has never been able to buy such another window, and has not ever since, either from books or men, heard any rumour at all of Golden Dragon City.

EPILOGUE

HERE the fourteenth Episode of the Book of Wonder endeth and here the relating of the Chronicles of Little Adventures at the Edge of the World. I take farewell of my readers. But it may be we shall even meet again, for it is still to be told how the gnomes robbed the fairies, and of the vengeance that the fairies took, and how even the gods themselves were troubled thereby in their sleep; and how the King of Ool insulted the troubadours, thinking himself safe among his scores of archers and hundreds of halberdiers, and how the troubadours stole to his towers by night, and under his battlements by the light of the moon made that king ridiculous for ever in song. But for this I must first return to the Edge of the World. Behold, the caravans start.

The Codes Of Hammurabi And Moses
W. W. Davies

QTY

The discovery of the Hammurabi Code is one of the greatest achievements of archaeology, and is of paramount interest, not only to the student of the Bible, but also to all those interested in ancient history...

Religion   **ISBN:** *1-59462-338-4*   **Pages:132**
MSRP $12.95

The Theory of Moral Sentiments
Adam Smith

QTY

This work from 1749. contains original theories of conscience amd moral judgment and it is the foundation for systemof morals.

Philosophy ISBN: *1-59462-777-0*   **Pages:536**
MSRP $19.95

Jessica's First Prayer
Hesba Stretton

QTY

In a screened and secluded corner of one of the many railway-bridges which span the streets of London there could be seen a few years ago, from five o'clock every morning until half past eight, a tidily set-out coffee-stall, consisting of a trestle and board, upon which stood two large tin cans, with a small fire of charcoal burning under each so as to keep the coffee boiling during the early hours of the morning when the work-people were thronging into the city on their way to their daily toil...

Pages:84

Childrens   ISBN: *1-59462-373-2*   **MSRP $9.95**

My Life and Work
Henry Ford

QTY

Henry Ford revolutionized the world with his implementation of mass production for the Model T automobile. Gain valuable business insight into his life and work with his own auto-biography... "We have only started on our development of our country we have not as yet, with all our talk of wonderful progress, done more than scratch the surface. The progress has been wonderful enough but..."

Pages:300

Biographies/   ISBN: *1-59462-198-5*   **MSRP $21.95**

www.bookjungle.com *email: sales@bookjungle.com fax: 630-214-0564 mail: Book Jungle PO Box 2226 Champaign, IL 61825*

The Art of Cross-Examination
Francis Wellman

QTY

I presume it is the experience of every author, after his first book is published upon an important subject, to be almost overwhelmed with a wealth of ideas and illustrations which could readily have been included in his book, and which to his own mind, at least, seem to make a second edition inevitable. Such certainly was the case with me; and when the first edition had reached its sixth impression in five months, I rejoiced to learn that it seemed to my publishers that the book had met with a sufficiently favorable reception to justify a second and considerably enlarged edition. ..

Pages:412

Reference   ISBN: *1-59462-647-2*   *MSRP $19.95*

On the Duty of Civil Disobedience
Henry David Thoreau

QTY

Thoreau wrote his famous essay, On the Duty of Civil Disobedience, as a protest against an unjust but popular war and the immoral but popular institution of slave-owning. He did more than write—he declined to pay his taxes, and was hauled off to gaol in consequence. Who can say how much this refusal of his hastened the end of the war and of slavery ?

Law   ISBN: *1-59462-747-9*   **Pages:48**

MSRP $7.45

Dream Psychology Psychoanalysis for Beginners
Sigmund Freud

QTY

Sigmund Freud, born Sigismund Schlomo Freud (May 6, 1856 - September 23, 1939), was a Jewish-Austrian neurologist and psychiatrist who co-founded the psychoanalytic school of psychology. Freud is best known for his theories of the unconscious mind, especially involving the mechanism of repression; his redefinition of sexual desire as mobile and directed towards a wide variety of objects; and his therapeutic techniques, especially his understanding of transference in the therapeutic relationship and the presumed value of dreams as sources of insight into unconscious desires.

Pages:196

Psychology   ISBN: *1-59462-905-6*   *MSRP $15.45*

The Miracle of Right Thought
Orison Swett Marden

QTY

Believe with all of your heart that you will do what you were made to do. When the mind has once formed the habit of holding cheerful, happy, prosperous pictures, it will not be easy to form the opposite habit. It does not matter how improbable or how far away this realization may see, or how dark the prospects may be, if we visualize them as best we can, as vividly as possible, hold tenaciously to them and vigorously struggle to attain them, they will gradually become actualized, realized in the life. But a desire, a longing without endeavor, a yearning abandoned or held indifferently will vanish without realization.

Pages:360

Self Help   ISBN: *1-59462-644-8*   *MSRP $25.45*

QTY

☐	**The Rosicrucian Cosmo-Conception Mystic Christianity** *by Max Heindel* ISBN: *1-59462-188-8* **$38.95** *The Rosicrucian Cosmo-conception is not dogmatic, neither does it appeal to any other authority than the reason of the student. It is; not controversial, but is; sent forth in the, hope that it may help to clear...* New Age/Religion Pages 646
☐	**Abandonment To Divine Providence** *by Jean-Pierre de Caussade* ISBN: *1-59462-228-0* **$25.95** *"The Rev. Jean Pierre de Caussade was one of the most remarkable spiritual writers of the Society of Jesus in France in the 18th Century. His death took place at Toulouse in 1751. His works have gone through many editions and have been republished...* Inspirational/Religion Pages 400
☐	**Mental Chemistry** *by Charles Haanel* ISBN: *1-59462-192-6* **$23.95** *Mental Chemistry allows the change of material conditions by combining and appropriately utilizing the power of the mind. Much like applied chemistry creates something new and unique out of careful combinations of chemicals the mastery of mental chemistry...* New Age Pages 354
☐	**The Letters of Robert Browning and Elizabeth Barret Barrett 1845-1846 vol II** ISBN: *1-59462-193-4* **$35.95** *by Robert Browning and Elizabeth Barrett* Biographies Pages 596
☐	**Gleanings In Genesis (volume I)** *by Arthur W. Pink* ISBN: *1-59462-130-6* **$27.45** *Appropriately has Genesis been termed "the seed plot of the Bible" for in it we have, in germ form, almost all of the great doctrines which are afterwards fully developed in the books of Scripture which follow...* Religion/Inspirational Pages 420
☐	**The Master Key** *by L. W. de Laurence* ISBN: *1-59462-001-6* **$30.95** *In no branch of human knowledge has there been a more lively increase of the spirit of research during the past few years than in the study of Psychology, Concentration and Mental Discipline. The requests for authentic lessons in Thought Control, Mental Discipline and...* New Age/Business Pages 422
☐	**The Lesser Key Of Solomon Goetia** *by L. W. de Laurence* ISBN: *1-59462-092-X* **$9.95** *This translation of the first book of the "Lemegeton" which is now for the first time made accessible to students of Talismanic Magic was done, after careful collation and edition, from numerous Ancient Manuscripts in Hebrew, Latin, and French...* New Age/Occult Pages 92
☐	**Rubaiyat Of Omar Khayyam** *by Edward Fitzgerald* ISBN:*1-59462-332-5* **$13.95** *Edward Fitzgerald, whom the world has already learned, in spite of his own efforts to remain within the shadow of anonymity, to look upon as one of the rarest poets of the century, was born at Bredfield, in Suffolk, on the 31st of March, 1809. He was the third son of John Purcell...* Music Pages 172
☐	**Ancient Law** *by Henry Maine* ISBN: *1-59462-128-4* **$29.95** *The chief object of the following pages is to indicate some of the earliest ideas of mankind, as they are reflected in Ancient Law, and to point out the relation of those ideas to modern thought.* Religion/History Pages 452
☐	**Far-Away Stories** *by William J. Locke* ISBN: *1-59462-129-2* **$19.45** *"Good wine needs no bush, but a collection of mixed vintages does. And this book is just such a collection. Some of the stories I do not want to remain buried for ever in the museum files of dead magazine-numbers an author's not unpardonable vanity..."* Fiction Pages 272
☐	**Life of David Crockett** *by David Crockett* ISBN: *1-59462-250-7* **$27.45** *"Colonel David Crockett was one of the most remarkable men of the times in which he lived. Born in humble life, but gifted with a strong will, an indomitable courage, and unremitting perseverance..* Biographies/New Age Pages 424
☐	**Lip-Reading** *by Edward Nitchie* ISBN: *1-59462-206-X* **$25.95** *Edward B. Nitchie, founder of the New York School for the Hard of Hearing, now the Nitchie School of Lip-Reading, Inc, wrote "LIP-READING Principles and Practice". The development and perfecting of this meritorious work on lip-reading was an undertaking...* How-to Pages 400
☐	**A Handbook of Suggestive Therapeutics, Applied Hypnotism, Psychic Science** ISBN: *1-59462-214-0* **$24.95** *by Henry Munro* Health/New Age/Health/Self-help Pages 376
☐	**A Doll's House: and Two Other Plays** *by Henrik Ibsen* ISBN: *1-59462-112-8* **$19.95** *Henrik Ibsen created this classic when in revolutionary 1848 Rome. Introducing some striking concepts in playwriting for the realist genre, this play has been studied the world over.* Fiction/Classics/Plays 308
☐	**The Light of Asia** *by sir Edwin Arnold* ISBN: *1-59462-204-3* **$13.95** *In this poetic masterpiece, Edwin Arnold describes the life and teachings of Buddha. The man who was to become known as Buddha to the world was born as Prince Gautama of India but he rejected the worldly riches and abandoned the reigns of power when...* Religion/History/Biographies Pages 170
☐	**The Complete Works of Guy de Maupassant** *by Guy de Maupassant* ISBN: *1-59462-157-8* **$16.95** *"For days and days, nights and nights, I had dreamed of that first kiss which was to consecrate our engagement, and I knew not on what spot I should put my lips..."* Fiction/Classics Pages 240
☐	**The Art of Cross-Examination** *by Francis L. Wellman* ISBN: *1-59462-309-0* **$26.95** *Written by a renowned trial lawyer, Wellman imparts his experience and uses case studies to explain how to use psychology to extract desired information through questioning...* How-to/Science/Reference Pages 408
☐	**Answered or Unanswered?** *by Louisa Vaughan* ISBN: *1-59462-248-5* **$10.95** *Miracles of Faith in China* Religion Pages 112
☐	**The Edinburgh Lectures on Mental Science (1909)** *by Thomas* ISBN: *1-59462-008-3* **$11.95** *This book contains the substance of a course of lectures recently given by the writer in the Queen Street Hall, Edinburgh. Its purpose is to indicate the Natural Principles governing the relation between Mental Action and Material Conditions...* New Age/Psychology Pages 148
☐	**Ayesha** *by H. Rider Haggard* ISBN: *1-59462-301-5* **$24.95** *Verily and indeed it is the unexpected that happens! Probably if there was one person upon the earth from whom the Editor of this, and of a certain previous history, did not expect to hear again...* Classics Pages 380
☐	**Ayala's Angel** *by Anthony Trollope* ISBN: *1-59462-352-X* **$29.95** *The two girls were both pretty, but Lucy who was twenty-one who supposed to be simple and comparatively unattractive, whereas Ayala was credited, as her Bombwhat romantic name might show, with poetic charm and a taste for romance. Ayala when her father died was nineteen...* Fiction Pages 484
☐	**The American Commonwealth** *by James Bryce* ISBN: *1-59462-286-8* **$34.45** *An interpretation of American democratic political theory. It examines political mechanics and society from the perspective of Scotsman James Bryce* Politics Pages 572
☐	**Stories of the Pilgrims** *by Margaret P. Pumphrey* ISBN: *1-59462-116-0* **$17.95** *This book explores pilgrims religious oppression in England as well as their escape to Holland and eventual crossing to America on the Mayflower; and their early days in New England...* History Pages 268

QTY

The Fasting Cure *by Sinclair Upton*   ISBN: *1-59462-222-1*   **$13.95**
In the Cosmopolitan Magazine for May, 1910, and in the Contemporary Review (London) for April, 1910, I published an article dealing with my experi-
ences in fasting. I have written a great many magazine articles, but never one which attracted so much attention...   New Age/Self Help/Health Pages 164

Hebrew Astrology *by Sepharial*   ISBN: *1-59462-308-2*   **$13.45**
In these days of advanced thinking it is a matter of common observation that we have left many of the old landmarks behind and that we are now pressing
forward to greater heights and to a wider horizon than that which represented the mind-content of our progenitors...   Astrology Pages 144

Thought Vibration or The Law of Attraction in the Thought World   ISBN: *1-59462-127-6*   **$12.95**
by William Walker Atkinson   Psychology/Religion Pages 144

Optimism *by Helen Keller*   ISBN: *1-59462-108-X*   **$15.95**
Helen Keller was blind, deaf, and mute since 19 months old, yet famously learned how to overcome these handicaps, communicate with the world, and
spread her lectures promoting optimism. An inspiring read for everyone...   Biographies/Inspirational Pages 84

Sara Crewe *by Frances Burnett*   ISBN: *1-59462-360-0*   **$9.45**
In the first place, Miss Minchin lived in London. Her home was a large, dull, tall one, in a large, dull square, where all the houses were alike, and all the
sparrows were alike, and where all the door-knockers made the same heavy sound...   Childrens/Classic Pages 88

The Autobiography of Benjamin Franklin *by Benjamin Franklin*   ISBN: *1-59462-135-7*   **$24.95**
The Autobiography of Benjamin Franklin has probably been more extensively read than any other American historical work, and no other book of its kind
has had such ups and downs of fortune. Franklin lived for many years in England, where he was agent...   Biographies/History Pages 332

Name	
Email	
Telephone	
Address	
City, State ZIP	

☐ **Credit Card**   ☐ **Check / Money Order**

Credit Card Number	
Expiration Date	
Signature	

Please Mail to: Book Jungle
                  PO Box 2226
                  Champaign, IL 61825
or Fax to: 630-214-0564

ORDERING INFORMATION

web: *www.bookjungle.com*
email: *sales@bookjungle.com*
fax: *630-214-0564*
mail: *Book Jungle PO Box 2226 Champaign, IL 61825*
or PayPal *to sales@bookjungle.com*

Please contact us for bulk discounts

DIRECT-ORDER TERMS

**20% Discount if You Order
Two or More Books**
Free Domestic Shipping!
Accepted: Master Card, Visa,
Discover, American Express

www.ingramcontent.com/pod-product-compliance
Lightning Source LLC
Chambersburg PA
CBHW080836250626
47160CB00008B/2950